Ghost Therapy

by

Mark Rosendorf

The Haunting of
Pinedale High Series

The Wild Rose Press, Inc.
PO Box 708
Adams Basin, NY 14410-0708
Visit us at www.thewildrosepress.com

Publishing History
First Edition, 2024
Trade Print ISBN 978-1-5092-5823-9
Digital ISBN 978-1-5092-5822-2

The Haunting of Pinedale High Series
Published in the United States of America

Dedication

To my wife, my family, and my students.
Also, to the ghosts in my school who may or may not
be there.

The following is the first book in the collaborative
series by the YA authors of The Wild Rose Press titled:
The Haunting of Pinedale High
Get ready as we take you on a fun and wild ride…

Chapter One

My mom named me Sam, short for Samuel. But if you hung around my high school, you'd think my name was "Loser", "Underwear", or "Jeri Curl". Every single morning, I had to wake up in my small apartment building on the poorer side of our small town and then walk five-and-a-half miles in rain or shine. I did this just to endure an entire day at Pinedale Central High School. Or, as a lot of students and graduates called it, Haunted High School.

It's called Haunted High School because, for years, students claimed they'd heard voices in the hallways. A few even insisted they saw shadowy figures floating around. One kid, like, ten years ago, said a ghost took over his body. That boy eventually jumped off the school's roof. To this day, adults say he was just some crazy kid suffering from depression and mental issues. His tale made for a great story every single Halloween or during camping trips in the woods.

Sometimes I wished I was a ghost. Then I wouldn't be three inches off the ground, hanging from my underwear outside the school's entranceway. Students like me called it "Haunted High School" for another reason. We've been haunted by the bigger, tougher kids who get their laughs at our expense. They're the evil spirits we're forced to run and hide from every day. Apparently the "no bully zone" rules talked about on the television haven't made their way to the town of Pinedale, at least not yet.

I never understood why Kurt Baker, the bully holding me up by my underwear, chose me as his constant target. I wasn't Kurt's only target, but I was his favorite. It could have been the color of my skin which made me stand out in a mostly white town like Pinedale. Or maybe it was that we were the same age, yet he was twice my size and about a hundred pounds heavier. It would be a huge deal except just about everyone my age was a lot bigger and bulkier than me, even most of the girls. But they weren't all pompous jerks who needed everyone's attention like Kurt. He could have chosen anyone to bully, but he picked me, and he did so every day. Maybe I was just lucky like that.

"Come on, Underwear, dance for us!" Kurt's command caught the attention of at least half a dozen of our schoolmates who were also on their way to the building. "Show them you're a good little puppet!"

I waved my arms and legs in the air, hoping if I did what he asked, this humiliation would end sooner rather than later. Two girls standing a distance away stared at me with wide eyes filled with sympathy. The girl and several boys close to us laughed loudly. One even clapped as if he was at the circus or something. I honestly wasn't sure which reaction was worse.

"That's enough!" an angry, gruff voice shouted from the building's front steps. "The school is officially open for the day. Everyone inside!"

"See you later, Loser," Kurt roared.

My feet hit the ground hard. Kurt jogged toward the school with his arms out as if he had just achieved an amazing victory. The other students waltzed past me while I was staggering to stay upright. No one offered me any help, but I didn't expect them to. It wasn't like any of them were my friends, or even wanted to get to know me.

I shoved my hands in my pants to pull the underwear out of my crack. A few of the students looked my way and giggled as they passed. I never really got why anyone, let alone almost everyone, stuck by Kurt and even cheered him on when he attacked me. Maybe it was because none of them wanted to become his next victim. Okay, so maybe I did get it.

Once I was "straightened out," I dropped to my knees and picked up my green knapsack. It rained last night, which meant the ground's moisture was now all over my bag. As I picked up the knapsack and tossed it over my shoulder, a shadow covered me. I lifted my head and looked over my shoulder, praying it wasn't Kurt coming back to force me to finish the show. Instead, it was Principal Bronson. That may not have been much better.

"Mister Anderson," he grunted through his thick, black mustache, "how long are you going to allow yourself to be that boy's clown?"

I couldn't help but laugh. His question sounded as if he thought I had a choice in the matter. It took me a moment to realize Principal Bronson was waiting for an answer. I didn't really have one and my huge grin wouldn't get me out of this conversation. "What can I do?" I asked, with a shrug.

"You can stand up to him! Earn his respect." Bronson's voice growled like an angry lion, as was always his way. "Didn't your father ever teach you how to fight for yourself?"

I shook my head back and forth. My father left Pinedale back when I was a year old. Whatever he taught me, I couldn't remember. My mom was my teacher on a lot of subjects, but nothing about fighting. Mostly, she told me to face everything in life with a smile and focus on the things that excite me. I'm sure Mom didn't spend her childhood getting lifted in the air by her underwear.

"It is called self-respect, son, and we all must have it in order to survive in this world." Bronson about-faced and walked away from me. "Now, go get your breakfast; classes begin in twenty-five minutes."

Funny, when I entered Pinedale High School last year and saw Principal Bronson for the first time, I thought he would treat me just a bit better than the other students. Maybe show me some favor due to our similar complexions. There were so few of us in this town, after all. As it turned out, he looked at me the same way he looked at everyone else, just another student for him to yell at. No wonder his three kids went to a private school outside of Pinedale; it was probably their choice.

I took a deep breath and looked around the grounds. We weren't far from acres and acres of cornfields, but that described everywhere in Pinedale, which was surrounded by cornfields on three sides. From the outside, no one would ever believe there was actual life here, with stores, schools, and streets between all those stalks of corn. Okay, enough thought on this lame town. Time to start my day.

I hopped up the school steps two at a time and entered through the double doors. A main vestibule led to three separate hallways and two creaky staircases which shared the same musty smell. They were all behind the circular desk where two safety officers stared at monitors while ignoring us. I could have gone down the staircase on the far right and into the cafeteria where I would be lost among a sea of students. Since my mom couldn't pay for the school food, I didn't have a reason to go there for breakfast.

Instead, I climbed the flight of steps on the left side of the circular desk. One floor up, and a walk down the hallway, led me to the library. The library was nice and quiet in the mornings. Not too many students liked to hang out in there, not when all the action was in the cafeteria. Here was a nice place to shake off my morning humiliations and begin my day. Considering the abuse always continued in the cafeteria, I don't know why I never went to the library during breakfast period before.

The library's glass door was in the middle of being cleaned by the custodian who ran a squeegee from top to bottom. A clear spray bottle hung from his left hand. I politely waited for him to finish. He looked back at me, then pulled open the door so I could walk through. "Here ya go, kid," he said.

"Thanks, Hank," I replied, then stepped through.

Hank smiled and nodded. Nice guy, but despite his friendliness, I was sure he didn't know me from any other student since he called all of us "Kid". I guess that was fair since no one really knew anything about him, either. With his grayish-balding hair, wide brown eyes, and baggy gray overalls, it was hard to guess his age. Seriously, the guy could have been somewhere between thirty and eighty. All I did know about him was that he had been cleaning messes in this building for a long time, maybe even since before I was born.

The librarian looked much older, but also a lot less friendly than Hank. She was famous for flipping out over any sort of noise. Knowing that, I entered the room then pushed the door closed as easily and as quietly as I could. Sure enough, the short, plump lady sat at the desk next to the door, staring at her computer screen through thick wide-rimmed glasses that hung near her nostrils. I threw her a friendly wave. She never looked up. I walked to the nearest of four rectangular tables in the middle of the room and unzipped my knapsack. Inside, I had a brown paper bag which contained my breakfast that I made myself, a fried egg and cheese on white toast. I also had a can of grape soda I picked up on my way to school.

To my surprise, the librarian and I weren't the only ones in the room, which I didn't expect this early in the morning. Britney Labelle, Kurt's girlfriend, and my least favorite girl in the world, sat in a chair at a nearby table. She had a binder open in front of her while tapping a pen against one of the metal rings. She was deep in studious thought, which was a rare sight, but it did explain the loud sigh that came out of her throat. Her dyed purple hair matched her blouse. That, along with way too much mascara, wasn't such a rare sight; it was her usual look, except for the coordinated colors that changed each week.

Britney wasn't alone. Two girls stood, one on each side, staring over her shoulder at the binder. The one on the right, I knew well. It was Britney's best friend, Paige Wheeler. Paige had been my friend up until the sixth grade, before her family moved across town. She wasn't the same person when we met again in high school.

Once here, I learned that Paige had become Britney's social project, and part of the school's coffeehouse clique. Meanwhile, I became Kurt's punchline for his never-ending joke. After that, Paige's friendliness toward me changed just like her hair color, which was now hot pink. To this day, Paige had no idea how often Britney trashed her behind her back.

Paige was a new and far worse person since moving to the Coffeehouse side of Pinedale. Coffeehouse was a name people dubbed that part of town because it had the only coffee house in Pinedale. A lot of nice homes with front yards were spread out all over that side. There was also a shopping mall which was built a few years back. Britney, Paige, and Kurt all lived on the Coffeehouse side of town. So did Principal Bronson and most of the teachers.

I lived on the third floor of Pinedale's one high rise apartment building a few miles away from the farms and the newish ranch-style houses which were built around the same time as the mall. I had no idea who lived in those, if anyone yet, but they stood out from being the only new buildings on our side of the town.

People called us The Bodega side because we had Pinedale's only convenience store and deli on the corner of our street. It was owned and run by the Santana family who had been in the town even longer than I'd been living here, and that was my entire life. They named it "The Bodega". The place even had a huge ugly sign above the front door with that name on it.

I never really knew what the word "Bodega" meant. It was a question I asked Mr. Santana a few times whenever I was in there. He'd always laugh at the question and say his padre, who came from Queens, named it. Now it was the unofficial name of our side of Pinedale. I had no doubt the name was chosen by the people on the Coffeehouse side, and it wasn't meant in a kind, neighborly way. We also had Sullivan's Discount Clothing store near The Bodega, it was where my mom got me the blue button-down collared shirt I had on. Too bad we weren't named after that. Then we could have been called the Sullivan side of town. That sounded much cooler to me.

"Ugh!" Britney slammed a hand against the table next to her notebook. "I can't believe I have to go in front of the class and talk about this stupid crap."

"You've had three weeks to put your presentation together, Brit," Paige sang in her high-pitched squeal. Her shoulder length pink hair swung as she turned away from her friend. "You're the one who waited until now. At least it's an easy project, right?"

"Easy?" Britney threw Paige a hard glare. "I have to talk about Pinedale's forest life and ideas on how to preserve it." She threw her hands in the air, and then on top of her head. "I didn't even know we had a forest around here! All I see are cornfields on every freakin' side of this stupid town—"

"Brit, we do have forest. It's behind the cornfields!" Paige's shouting led to a "shush" from the librarian. She tossed the librarian a thumbs-up.

"The first farmers in Pinedale," Paige whispered, "sliced out half the forest to make those cornfields."

"Oh my God, how do you even know that?"

"Girl, I live here. So do you." Paige slapped Britney's shoulder. "How do you *not* know that?

Seriously, check out some of your town besides clothing stores in the mall."

"I like the mall," Britney snapped with an eyeroll.

The third girl, looking over Britney's left shoulder, let out a huge cackle. She was a girl I'd never seen in the school, or in town, before. If I had, surely, I'd have remembered those long, brown braids that hung over both shoulders and past her belly. And the dress that covered her arms to her wrists and draped down to her toes—it looked like something from that old TV-show, Little House on...something. I didn't know any girls still wore those... Well, not until this one.

But what really stood out to me was the fact that I could see the stocked bookshelves behind her. Somehow, I was seeing everything behind this girl as if I was looking through her. It was like she was there, but she wasn't. It was actually kind of cool although I didn't know how she was doing it, or why she was dressed like someone from the early nineteen hundreds or whenever. Halloween was a few months back and there weren't any themed parties in the school or the town, at least none I knew about, or was invited to. I couldn't help myself; I had to ask.

I ran up to the table, facing the three girls. I gazed directly at the strange one. "I don't mean to be, like, rude or nothing, but where did you get that old-fashioned dress?"

Britney and Paige lifted their heads from the textbook and eyed me with the usual faces of disdain. "What the hell are you talking about, Loser?" Britney growled.

"Not you. Her." I pointed at the strange girl that, as I stood closer, I really could see through her. What was the word we learned in science class…transparent. Yeah, that was it. This girl was transparent. "Do you two know her? How is she doing that?"

Paige peered around the library, then back at me. "Her who, Sam? Doing what?"

The strange girl's eyes went wide. With a huge smile across her face, she asked me one strange question. In fact, it was the strangest question I had ever been asked in my entire life.

"You can really see me?"

Chapter Two

"You see what Kurt is saying, Paige?" Britney said with a huge eyeroll. "This boy *is* a total freak."

Paige nudged a hand toward the door. "How about we finish this in the caf? We'll get more privacy down there."

Britney snatched her notebook from the table and followed Paige out of the library. I watched them leave, then waltzed around the table toward the one girl left, the transparent one in old-fashioned clothes. I stopped in place, facing her, but just out of reach. It was so weird. The girl stood in front of me, but her entire body was like I was looking through a water bottle. I reached out to touch her shoulder. My hand went straight through. I yanked it back as if I had just stuck my fingers in an open flame.

I stared at my hand which had a slight chill to it. It could have been because I put it through a girl that wasn't there. Or maybe it was just my nerves. Maybe the talk about ghosts in the school was true? I didn't think anyone really believed that, but I couldn't think of another explanation off the top of my head. I guess she could have been a magician or something. But I was only inches away from her and if this was a trick, I'd see...I don't know...a projector or something?

She stared at me with a smirk across her face.

"Are you...a ghost?" I asked.

"I'm Jessica." She had a bit of an accent. It wasn't British, not really. It was more an old-style English, like from those movies I used to watch with my grandpa. The ones without color. "Some people call me Jess. Your name is Sam, right?"

My mouth hit the floor. "You know my name?"

"Yes, I like to people-watch." Her tongue rolled across her upper lip. "To be honest, that's all the entertainment I have to keep me busy."

I dropped my head. That's when I noticed her feet—which were covered in old fashioned black farmer boots—were at least three inches from the library's tiled floor. The girl wasn't standing; she was floating. My gaze drifted to the ceiling. There were no wires or anything holding her off the floor. No, she was floating in mid-air.

I had in front of me real proof the school really was haunted, and it was haunted, not just by the bullies, but by a ghost named Jessica. A dead girl right now stood in front of me, and we were talking. There was only one way I could react in this situation.

"Oh my God, this is so cool!" I threw my arms in the air. "You're really a ghost! Like, an actual ghost! I can't believe it—"

"Excuse me!" the librarian shouted from her desk. "This is a library, young man. If you insist on talking to yourself, please do so at no more than a whisper."

"Sorry!" I leaned forward and said in my lowest voice possible, "She can't see or hear you?"

Jessica shrugged. "I haven't met a single adult who could."

"Whoa."

I bolted behind the nearest bookcase, hoping

Jessica would follow me. Seeing her phase through the bookcase and stop in front of me nearly knocked me over. "This is so cool. You're an actual ghost." My body shivered with excitement. "Everyone says the school is haunted. Has it been you all this time?"

She looked up at the ceiling in thought. She nodded, then looked back at me. "I've never seen another one, but I've heard students in the past talk about ghosts. A lot of times, they said 'he', so they couldn't have meant me. I am sure I don't resemble a boy."

"No, not at all." I bit the tip of my tongue to keep from cracking up. The last thing I wanted to do was be disrespectful. "So, there are more ghosts?"

"I suppose so. One time, I did see a boy act possessed. I didn't do it, though. I swear."

"Ooh!" I waved a finger at Jessica. "You're talking about Edward Ross, the kid who jumped off the roof like, twenty-something years ago, right?"

"Has it been that long?" Her head tilted. "Maybe, I can't tell. Every day is the same for me."

"But you're sure he was possessed?"

She flew around me. I spun in a 180 to face her. "Eddie was able to see me. That was the last time anyone could. He told me he talked to another ghost. He said it was a boy ghost. All I do know is that, in the last week before Eddie died, he just wasn't acting like himself. All of a sudden, he couldn't see or hear me anymore."

I cupped a hand over my mouth. This was so weird, but also so amazing. Ghosts at Pinedale Central High School were real, and there wasn't just one. It sounded like they couldn't see or hear each other, or at least Jessica couldn't.

"Do you want to know the weird thing, Sam?" Jessica thrust her hands forward. "I tried to stop Eddie from jumping. Even though he was no longer responding to me, I still felt I had to try. In his last moment, he pushed me out of the way, then jumped. No one had ever been able to touch me before."

"That does sound weird." I reached out and my hand went through her again. Not a big surprise, but I had to make sure at least one more time. We'd have to hit that Eddie Ross topic again. Right now, I had so many more questions to ask. "So, you're actually from Pinedale? Like, you went to school here?" I brought my hands together and rotated them in a circle. "I mean, when you were alive."

"Yes, Sam, I did." She waved four fingers toward the window. "My family ran the farm out yonder. We lived there, as well."

"Which farm?"

Her eyes narrowed with confusion. "There's more than one?"

"Oh, yeah, there's three! Wow, this is so—"

A hand tapped the back of my neck. I nearly jumped out of my skin as I looked over my shoulder. For a brief moment, I thought it was Kurt ready to grab my underwear and yank me off the floor again. Lucky for me, it was just the librarian.

"Young man," she barked. "It is almost eight o'clock, which means you will soon be late for your first period class. Please finish up your, um...conversation and make your way to where you're supposed to be."

"Oh, I didn't realize." I glanced back at Jessica.

"Sorry."

The librarian stormed off. Jessica laughed, which made my grin grow until my lips almost touched my ears. "The adults really can't see you," I whispered.

"Most of the students can't either, only the ones that are special."

I placed my hand against my chest. "Are you saying I'm special?"

She smiled. "It sure looks that way to me."

Even though I had just met her, Jessica's compliment made me feel good. I had a feeling she had been a ghost in this school for a long time, and, as she said, only a few of us who were special could talk to her. I was one of them. That made me special.

"This is so cool. You're really a ghost."

"Do you realize this is the third time you have said that?" Jessica flashed another smirk. I threw up my arms and shrugged.

Man, I had so many more questions, and Jessica may have been the coolest person I'd ever met. That wasn't just because she was a ghost. I decided to take a chance. "Hey, do you want to, um, hang out or something at my place after school? It's not too big, but there's a park nearby."

"You're so sweet, Sam. I wish I could." Jessica's head shook back and forth. "But I can't leave the school."

"Why not? Are there rules you have to follow? Do you get in trouble if you do?"

"No. I mean I literally cannot leave the building."

I raised my eyebrows. "Have you tried?"

She threw me a glance that called my question stupid.

"Oh. Okay, I get it now." I really didn't get it, but this didn't sound like a brushoff so it must have been true. "Why can't you leave the building?"

"I don't know, Sam. I'm a ghost, not a ghost expert."

"But you are a ghost. You must have some idea—"

"Why would I, silly boy?" She waved her fingers at my sneakers. "Do you know why your feet move when you want to walk?"

Hmm, good point. Walking wasn't something I ever thought about; it was just something I did, and have been able to do for as long as I could remember. I guess being a ghost was just something she did, too.

"In that case, can we hang out here tomorrow morning? I'll bring breakfast."

She nodded with a grin. "I'll be here."

"Young man!" The librarian's shout echoed throughout the room.

"I gotta go." I backpedaled a few steps. "Wow, this is—"

"—so cool. I know."

I waved to her, then ran around the bookcase. I snatched my knapsack along with the rest of my sandwich from the table and went for the door. I waved goodbye to the librarian, but she ignored me as if I was the ghost in the room.

I ran down the stairs to the first floor where I had my early morning class, which was social studies. I stopped in place when I noticed Kurt skipping through the hallway among the other students scurrying to their classes. His hands were behind his back, which was suspicious. I pushed myself against the wall in order to keep him from grabbing me from behind and lifting me by my underwear again. Of course, he went straight to me. We had everyone's attention.

Kurt pulled his right hand out from behind his back. In it was a pint-sized milk carton from the cafeteria. The top was completely ripped open. As Kurt passed, he slammed the carton into my crotch, soaking my pants. He walked off laughing along with all the giggles in the hallway from the other students around us.

Well, at least it was something new this time.

Chapter Three

Phys Ed used to be my favorite class of the day, at least it was last semester. That was before my schedule was changed and I now had the class at the end of the day…with Kurt. That meant each time I entered that locker room, there was a fifty-percent chance I would be lifted off the floor by my underwear for all the boys in the class to laugh. Or I'd get a sweaty pair of gym shorts thrown in my face. The underwear thing already happened once this morning and I didn't feel like a repeat performance. My pants were finally dry from the milk, so I decided to cut out and head home early.

It was a five-and-a-half-mile walk from the school to my apartment building on the Bodega side of town, but I didn't mind it. I really liked this town and all there was to see, even if it didn't always like me. I passed Lou's Diner just a few blocks from the school. So far, I had never eaten there, at least not yet. We couldn't afford to eat out much, but I promised myself that someday in the future I'd take my mom to Lou's and pay for dinner. A few miles later, I was walking up the hill that led to my area of Pinedale. It was the toughest part of the walk, in either direction, especially during bad weather.

I liked to stop once I hit the top of the hill and look to the east. It was there I had the best view of the Blue Ridge mountains that stood past the Pinedale woods.

My middle school teacher once told us that the Blue Ridge mountains were known and admired all over North Carolina, even if no one outside of Pinedale ever heard of us, the town closest to those mountains, and with the best view. One of my goals when I become an adult is to climb to the top of those mountains so I can touch the clouds.

Another half-mile and I hit our supermarket. The owners, an older couple who left Pinedale, then came back, were really nice people who gave out free samples of food. They liked my mom because she worked there part-time when she was younger. Many times, at the end of the day, the owner gave us frozen chicken and a few packaged foods for free, which helped us out a lot. He liked to call us "his favorite customers." That statement always brought a smile to my mom's face. Mine, too.

My only complaint was how crowded that supermarket could get, especially on weekends. Even people from the Coffeehouse side of town drove over there to shop. The prices were much cheaper than their supermarket. That's why Mom shopped there during the week whenever she could. Less crowded when everyone else was at work.

This was my side of Pinedale, and it was home. I rarely drifted to the Coffeehouse side of town. The mall over there didn't interest me. It was all designer clothes, a video game store, a movie theater, and a few other stores that were way too expensive for me, at least at this point in my life. I went to the mall's food court once earlier in the year but all I could afford was a hot pretzel for lunch. When I saw Kurt, Britney, and some of their friends hanging out at one of the tables, I left before they could see me. I never went back.

Finally, I made it to my block, famous for The Bodega on the corner. It shared the street with Sullivan's Discount Clothing store, Jack's Hardware Boutique, and the walk-in medical center where my mom worked behind the desk. Farther down was my apartment building standing all by its lonesome. I used one of my two keys to open the front door, then walked two flights up to my hallway. Apartment 3E was next to the stairs. I used the second key to enter my home.

I threw my knapsack on the hardwood table, then pushed the door closed. To my surprise, Mom walked out from the kitchen. A black hat covered her short hair. A white pocketbook hung from the strap over her right shoulder. It worked with her pink blouse, or at least I thought so. Funny, she carried so much stuff in that old pocketbook, it was actually wider than her thin frame.

"Mom, you're home," I said, with a cheese-faced smile.

"Yes, I'm on the evening shift tonight." She threw me a quizzical glance. "Why are you here so early? School ends at three, and it's three o'clock right now."

"Oh, our gym teacher is absent, so they let us go." I flashed a grin.

"Okay, I'll accept that explanation. This time." Mom walked around the table and dropped into one of our two metal chairs placed across from one another. They weren't exactly a matched set. "How about we talk a bit before I go?" She waved a hand at the other chair. I sat down and dropped my palms against the table.

"How are things going in school, Sammy?" she asked. "Is that huge boy still picking on you? What was his name?"

"Kurt Baker, and nah, it's all good, Mom."

"Are you sure?" She reached across the table and placed her hand over mine. "I could go to the school in the morning and have another chat with that principal of yours."

Ooh, that sounded like a bad idea, for sure. The last time Mom spoke to the principal, it didn't go well. Principal Bronson brought both Kurt and me into his office and made him apologize. For the next month, I was called "snitch" by all of his friends and for the next six days my breakfast sandwich was taken, then tossed in the garbage. That's why, as of this morning, I decided to eat breakfast in the library. It was the one place Kurt wouldn't go.

"It's okay, Mom." I shook my head back and forth. "I can handle that kid."

"I know school isn't the easiest place for you, Sammy." Mom's eyes watered. "I just want to be helpful and make things better."

"I know, and it is better, Mom. Honest." I ran a finger across my chest up and down, then left to right. It was my way of showing her I was telling the truth. Okay, I wasn't actually telling the truth, but I didn't want her to worry. "I even made a new friend today." At least that part was true.

"A new friend, you say?" Mom's back straightened against the chair. "That is good news. What's his name?"

"Actually…" My mouth stretched into an embarrassed grin. "Her name is Jessica."

"Jessica." Mom's smile suddenly matched mine. "Is this…"

"Oh, no, nothing like that." My cheeks were warm. "We're just good friends."

"'You never know. Things do change over time." Mom cupped her hands together. "So, what's she like?"

"Um…" What could I say about her besides the obvious? "She's a white girl—"

"Oh. Well, that's okay.

"She's also sort of old-fashioned. She wears a long dress to school."

"Really?" Mom's head tipped back. "I suppose there's nothing wrong with that. How did you meet Jessica?"

"Well, you know me." I jumped out of my chair and danced back and forth. I then spun in a circle and rotated my fists around each other. "Once I start showing off the moves, and putting a little dance into my step…"

"I know, no one can resist my baby boy." Mom leaned forward. "This Jessica…are you absolutely sure she's just a friend? Maybe she's interested in you, if you get my drift." Her eyes widened with excitement. I totally caught what she meant.

"I'm sure it's nothing like that, Mom. We're just friends. Jessica's not really…the touching type."

"Oh, so she's a shy girl. Well, give it some time, Sammy. You never know." Mom stood from her chair. "I must get to work. There's a piece of chicken and some corn in the fridge for you to heat up. Make sure to get your homework done. I'll be home by midnight. If you're still up by then, you can tell me more about Jessica."

"Sure thing, Mom." Although I wasn't sure how much more I could tell her. "It's complicated" didn't begin to describe her.

Chapter Four

I never had that conversation with Mom. I tried to wait up for her, but I guess I fell asleep. Before I knew it, my alarm went off telling me it was morning. Mom was still in her bedroom with the door closed, which meant she got home a lot later than she expected. I went through my routine which included taking a shower, making breakfast, and choosing a shirt to wear with my black jeans. Today, it was a blue short-sleeved buttoned shirt. I tiptoed around so I wouldn't wake Mom.

Now that I was ready, I headed to school early, looking forward to spending more time with my new "friend." I entered the building and went straight to the library. By doing this, I also managed to avoid seeing Kurt outside the school. Maybe I should come to school early every day.

So far, it was just me and the librarian. I had no idea what time she got here, but she looked like it had been a while. For all I knew, she could have lived in the library. She did sort of have that hermit look to her. The librarian threw me an annoyed glance, then typed away on her computer at her desk while I made my way to the same table I sat at yesterday morning.

From my knapsack, I took a brown paper bag which had my breakfast sandwich and a few napkins inside. I tossed the knapsack over the back of the chair. Then I waited for what felt like forever. According to the clock on the wall, it had only been five minutes. I thought I'd end up eating by myself, but then a forehead above a pair of eyes popped up through the table.

"Hello, Sam!" Jessica floated straight up and nearly touched the ceiling. Her body lowered through the table, stopping at her waist. My heart raced with thrill at seeing her. It wasn't an "in love" sort of feeling, I hadn't really started with all that yet. It was more about having a kind of friend that not too many others could claim.

"Heya, Jess." I reached into my brown paper bag. "I brought you something."

I took out another fried egg and cheese sandwich wrapped in a napkin. I placed it in front of her. "I made you some breakfast. I thought we could eat together. We had some extra bacon, so I put a slice in there for you."

Jessica chuckled. "That's so sweet, but truly unnecessary."

I felt my smile fade. "You don't like eggs, or is it the cheese?" I knew it couldn't be the bacon—who didn't love bacon?

"That's not the problem, Sam." She raised a hand and slowly dropped it down. It phased through the sandwich and the table's surface.

"Oh, you can't touch anything, can you?" To be honest, I felt kind of stupid in that moment.

"No, I can't. I've heard about other ghosts being able to touch and move things, but I never could."

"Oh. Okay, I get it, you're a ghost. You probably don't eat, right?"

"No, not at all." Jessica gave me a what was

25

obviously a pity smile. "But thank you, anyway. Please, eat. Don't let me spoil your appetite."

I picked up my sandwich with both hands and took a bite. It was weird having someone watch me eat without eating anything herself. Although it did happen more than a few times with Mom when she made one meal because that was all we had in the fridge and watched me eat it for supper. I always made a point to talk to her while I ate, just so it wouldn't be so awkward.

"So, Jess," I said, after a swallow, trying to do the same with her. "Any idea why we have ghosts in our school?" I wiped my mouth with the back of my hand. "You never hear about that happening anywhere else."

Jessica crossed her legs into a sitting position. She levitated inches above the table. "I've heard some theories over the years; the adults talk about it a lot in the staff lounge." Her hands folded in her lap. "Many of them think the ghost sightings are stories made up by students with stress who are either making up lies or it's happening only in their imagination."

I dropped my sandwich before I could take another bite. I looked over Jessica with widened eyes. There were days I was totally stressed. "Can that be right? Am I imagining you?"

"No, silly, I'm really here." Jessica rolled her eyes.

"Oh, well, that's good." I took another bite and chewed. I tasted the strip of bacon I put in my sandwich. It was so yummy...of course, it was bacon.

"There was one theory about a witch being buried here before the school was built. Another one, I heard a few teachers say, is that several of Carolina's ley lines meet here, and that's why we exist in the school, but nowhere else."

I swallowed. "What's a ley line?"

"Truth be told, I have no idea." Jessica laughed along with me. "There was a time, way back, when the students were obsessed with ghosts. The school brought in a ghost expert who spoke to everyone in the auditorium. He said that some of the dead exist as ghosts until they figure out what they were meant to do. Only then will they feel a pull that takes them to eternal rest."

"Do you think he was right?"

"He might be. He did say he was a ghost expert." Jessica's shoulders lifted. "Then again, I was on the stage a few feet from him the entire time and he had no idea I was there."

"Not much of an expert then." I swallowed another bite, then licked my lips. I had to wonder what made the guy a ghost expert. Did he have a degree in that or something? "If he's right, what do you think you're here to do?"

I expected another giggle out of Jessica. But when I looked up, she was staring at me hard and with a serious gaze across her face.

"What?" I asked.

After a few moments of silence, she spoke in a slow and deliberate tone, one adults used on me when they were explaining something they felt I needed to understand. "For the first time since my death, I think I may have an idea on why I am here."

"What idea?" I picked up my sandwich and stared at the brownish crust. "Why do you think you're here?"

"I think I'm still around because I'm supposed to help you, Sam. Maybe that's why you can see me when so many others cannot."

"You're here to help me?" I realized I'd squeezed my sandwich so hard, some of the egg and cheese slipped through the two pieces of cold toast and landed on the napkin. "Help me with what?"

"Stand up to that big fellow who does you harm."

Ugh, even here in the library, I couldn't escape the dark spirit of Kurt Baker. "You've seen that?"

"No one has missed it, Sam. Not the dead, and certainly not the living."

"I'm fine, Jess." I held out my palms and kicked my chair away from the table. "What he does, it's no big deal. It doesn't bother me as much. Not anymore."

Jessica's head tilted in a way that told me she saw through my lie just as I could see through her entire body. Her legs dropped from her sitting position and disappeared under the table. She sailed toward me. She finally stopped moving when we were eye to eye.

"I was picked on, same as you, when I was alive and attending this school." She nodded before I could ask if that was true. "It was by a boy named Rowland, and he was the headmaster's son."

"Headmaster?"

"Yes. That is what you now refer to as the principal. Back then, his title was headmaster, and he saw no evil in his offspring."

"What...what did Rowland do to you?"

Jessica lifted her head toward the ceiling. She spoke with her eyes closed. "He told everyone I was a witch, and soon, they all called me that. I remember one time he soaked me with a bucket of water. For reasons I never knew, I was this boy's fool."

Wow, I totally understood what that was like. I

stood from my seat. Jessica held out a hand like a stop sign telling me to keep listening. "I stood up to the boy, Sam. I faced my demon in front of all our classmates."

"How?" The word jumped off my tongue before I could stop it. She had my attention. "What did you do?"

"I punched him straight in the bellybutton!" Jessica propelled her fist forward. By instinct, I flinched. Her hand went straight through my chest. "Then, I challenged him to either leave me alone, or fight me in front of everyone."

I dropped back into my chair. "What did he do?"

"He just stared at me with a dumb look on his face." Jessica floated above me and clapped her hands together. "The others pointed and laughed at him. One even called Rowland a witch."

"Really? Then he backed off?" I had a hunch "witch" was a huge insult at the time.

Jessica nodded. "When he realized in that moment our classmates had turned against him, Rowland backed away. Then he ran off. From that moment forward, life at school changed. No one called me a witch again. Our classmates no longer sent cruelty my way. After that, everything went much better…" She let out a deep sigh. "That is, until the first fire which tore through the basement claimed my life."

I tipped my head. "There was more than one?"

At least now I had an idea why the cafeteria always had that burning smell to it. I always thought it was the kitchen scorching our food. My brain begged me to ask her about the fires, but that was a topic for another time. "Wow, I really wish I could stand up to Kurt like that."

"Why can you not?"

Jessica lunged. She passed through me. I jumped to

29

my feet and spun around to face her, accidentally knocking over the chair. "Um, because Kurt is so much bigger than me? He'd probably kill me on the spot. Then I'd be a ghost, too."

"I have been people-watching for a long time, Sam, a very long time." Jessica waved a hand toward the door. "People like him prey on the weak for the attention of others. They crave the laughs and the applause. They do so because, deep down, they are insecure. They are scared little boys, afraid of their own shadows."

She leaned in, bringing her nose up to mine. "Confront this Kurt fellow and you will turn the crowd against him. That is how you back him off. I have seen it happen many times before."

The idea of actually fighting Kurt gave me a massive stomachache. But if I didn't do something, he'd most likely pick on me until the day we graduated—and that meant another two-and-a-half years of torture. I've wanted to do something to get Kurt off my back since the first time he picked me up by my underwear. A fight wasn't what I had in mind, but when a ghost gives advice, who am I to ignore it?

But still…

"What if I challenge him to a fight and he kicks my ass?"

Jessica shrugged. "Then your reputation would be no worse off than it is now. True?"

Well, sure, nothing changes except getting my ass kicked. But as far as my reputation, I guess she had a point about that. "I'll…I'll think about what you're saying."

"Think hard, smart boy." Jessica smirked. She

reached over to pat me on the head. Of course, her hand couldn't actually touch my scalp.

"Excuse me, young man." The librarian stepped between us, facing me. "It is eight o'clock. Please pick up my chair and go to your first period class."

"Okay, Ms. Librarian. Sorry about the chair." I wrapped up what was left of my sandwich and tossed it in my knapsack along with the uneaten one I had made for Jessica. "Thanks for letting me know."

"If I may suggest something for you." The librarian stepped in my path to the door. "The town's clinic has excellent mental health workers there. You may want to speak with them."

I peeked over at Jessica. We cracked up until she left the room through the floor. The librarian backed away with a look of concern aimed my way.

Chapter Five

I spent the morning in my classes thinking about Jessica's advice. It matched the opinion everyone else gave me whether I asked for it or not. Now it was coming from a ghost that had been hanging around the school for at least a century and saw everything. Maybe there was something to it.

Would standing up to my bully change my life? I didn't like the idea. No. In truth, I was frightened by it...but nothing I had done so far to get Kurt to lay off had worked. It seemed the more he attacked me, the more our schoolmates enjoyed it, which made him harass me at every turn. Maybe this was the only way. It sure couldn't make things worse. Could it?

Lunchtime in the cafeteria didn't seem like the right place for the confrontation, not with so many students, staff, and chaos all over. Instead, I spent the period avoiding Kurt by staying on the opposite side of wherever he was sitting with Britney, Paige, and their collection of friends. The lunch period was about to end, and I'd stayed safe, but that wouldn't last forever. Kurt would eventually catch up to me. He couldn't help himself.

The school bell rang, signaling that the lunch period was over. It was time for our afternoon classes. I slowly walked the stairs to the first floor. The other students scurrying to their classes suddenly stopped in their tracks. I did the same just a few feet from my classroom. Some looked at me, others looked behind me. There were devious grins all around. The time to confront my bully was about to come.

I knew Kurt's demented cackle anywhere. I always heard it just before, and while, getting pulled off the floor from behind by my underwear. The laughter, and the eyes of the crowd, grew closer. I could have dashed into the classroom and put this off. But I decided to stay in the hallway. The moment had come to follow the ghost's advice. I tossed my knapsack off my shoulder and onto the floor. I took a deep breath, ready to try this.

I balled my right hand into a fist. But what could that do to a guy with a gut as huge as Kurt's? Not much at all. In fact, I had a feeling my fist wouldn't do damage at all except make him, and everyone else, laugh even harder. But what about my foot? Maybe.

I turned to see Kurt running my way with a huge grin across his face. He had too much momentum to stop. I planted my left foot against the floor and threw my right leg out straight. The sole of my white sneaker slammed into Kurt's stomach. Somehow, I kept my balance and didn't fall over. Kurt, however, exhaled a gulp of air. He hobbled two steps backward, and then fell onto his butt cheeks.

Kurt looked up at me with widened eyes. I know my kick didn't hurt him all that bad, but it sure did surprise him. I looked at the crowd of students and their open-mouthed, stunned faces. Then, after several silent seconds, the impossible happened. The crowd cheered. A few even clapped. Others—mostly the boys—looked down at Kurt and cracked up. Kurt's face lit up as if it was on fire.

"I'm tired of your crap, Kurt!" I shouted louder than I had ever shouted before. "If we need to fight to make it stop, then fine, I'm ready to fight!"

The cheering made my eardrums shake. In this moment, everything changed, just as Jessica said it would. The tables had turned. For the first time in my life, I had the spotlight, and I shined. The thrill made my heart flutter. No wonder Kurt enjoyed it as much as he did. Even as he climbed to his feet, I felt like I was the tall hero everyone looked up to, and he was the embarrassed wimp half my size.

At least, that was until Kurt's green eyes narrowed. His teeth ground like a rabid dog. The smile melted from my face. "Um, let's call a truce, okay?"

Kurt lunged at me. The right hand connecting with my jaw sent a shock down my entire body that I even felt in my toes. I flew backward and slammed into the wall. In all the time Kurt teased, bullied, harassed, and humiliated me, he never once hit me. Not until right now. He certainly threatened to, many times, but he never once actually did it. I always imagined his gigantic fist pounding my face would hurt. Wow, I was so right.

Before I could brace myself, two gorilla-like hands wrapped around my throat and pressed my body against the hard concrete. The cheers quickly turned into gasps. The laughter had stopped. I tried to suck in some air, but it was like trying to breathe underwater.

My throat burned like it was on fire. I wanted to speak, tell him I got the point, but only gagging sounds came out of my mouth. Through blurred vision and Kurt's high-pitched screams, I made out students pulling on his arms. Then it was adults—one teacher and two safety officers. Principal Bronson jumped in as well, screaming for people to clear the hallway.

Shrieks of panic sounded all around me. People cried. Others shouted, "Kurt, stop!"

I wasn't worried, though. Even if they couldn't pull him off me, I knew Kurt would eventually have to let me go. I just had to wait it out. He had to…right? Both of us had a math test tomorrow that we were told was worth half our grade. The new math teacher, Ms. Kouriki, didn't tolerate lateness, especially when she was giving a test. We had to pass it. Kurt for sure couldn't afford to fail, so he had to stop so we could get to class.

Above Kurt's head, I saw Jessica floating near the ceiling and staring down at me. Her eyes were wide. Her bottom lip shook. "I'm sorry," she sobbed. "I'm so, so sorry…" Wow, she was really upset. I'd have to ask her why later, after Kurt was finished showing off…

Then, just like that, the excitement was over.

I no longer had Kurt's fingers squeezing my throat. In fact, nothing hurt, no pain at all. I was fine, just as I knew I would be. I moved away from the wall. No matter how hard I tried, I couldn't remember when, exactly, he let me go, or how the fight stopped. But I was free, and nothing on me felt broken. Maybe I passed out at some point, yet I somehow stayed on my feet. In truth, I wasn't worried because I knew he'd have to stop.

Damn, so much for standing up to my bully. If anything, this was a win for the bully. I just hoped his attacks wouldn't get worse now.

The floor was clear of students, which I also didn't

see happen. A few adults lingered in the hallway, including Principal Bronson. His clothes were wrinkled, his tie was unwrapped and hanging over his shoulders. He was sweating along his bald head something fierce. I saw two men who I thought were safety officers kneeling over someone asleep on the floor.

As I moved closer, I realized they weren't safety officers at all. They were actual deputies from Pinedale's sheriff's office. Why were they here? The gray-haired lady crouching next to them wore a white jacket and had a stethoscope around her neck. She pulled a white sheet over the face of the person on the floor. I got a glance at the top of the person's head before the sheet fully covered him. It was a boy with a Jeri curled hairstyle just like mine. When did he start at this school? I know I never saw him, and the school wasn't all that big. What had happened to him? Did Kurt attack him after our fight? For me not to notice all this commotion, I must've been unconscious quite a while.

The lady looked up toward Principal Bronson, holding out her watch-wearing hand. "Time of death, I'm putting at approximately twelve thirty p.m. What did you say the boy's name was?"

"Anderson," Bronson answered. "Sam Anderson."

Wait, what? Did she say "time of…"

"Guys. That's not me, I'm right here!" I waved my hands to get their attention. I gasped realizing my hands were transparent, just like Jessica's whole body. My hand was in front of my face, yet I could still see Bronson and the police as clearly as if there was nothing between us. I gasped, then cried out for help. No one heard my screams. No one but me.

The door to the school counselor's office opened. The town sheriff and a deputy walked out with Kurt who had his head down and his hands behind his back. The deputy held Kurt by the arm. As they passed me, I saw the metal cuffs around Kurt's wrists.

Bronson stepped in front of Kurt. "Your mother and stepfather are going to meet you at the sheriff's office. I recommend you not a say word until they arrive. Understood?"

Kurt never looked up at Bronson; his eyes stayed on the floor. The officers led him through the hallway and toward the doors.

"Kurt!" I called. "What the hell? What did you do to me?"

Kurt looked up, then back and forth. He dropped his head back down. Did he hear me? Weird if he did because I was sure no one else heard me. It didn't matter. Kurt was taken out the door and from the school, hopefully forever.

Bronson and the lady with the white jacket who had just gotten to her feet looked at one another. "This is not good for us, not good at all," Bronson said to her. "We're about to have a PR nightmare."

The woman didn't answer. There was a sadness in the air I had felt once before, at my grandpa's funeral. Oh my God—

"Principal Bronson, what happened?" I shouted. "Did he, like, kill me? Am I dead?"

I didn't want to believe it, not until I looked down and realized my feet weren't touching the floor. The ceiling was about an inch above my head. I reached up to touch it, but my hand went straight through. "Okay, this is kind of cool."

My body passed through the plastered ceiling. I was now on the second floor near the library's entrance. There was no doubt, I was confused and needed help. I needed someone who could explain to me what was happening. My eyes panned to the library's wood door. I knew who could answer all my questions. I sure hoped I could find her in there.

"Jessica!" I screamed. I reached for the door, but couldn't move, not while I was floating in midair.

Chapter Six

My legs scurried through the air as if I was running on a treadmill. They moved fast but I wasn't going anywhere. I was stuck in one spot. My arms and legs flailed just as they did every time Kurt held me up by my underwear. I needed to calm down, and quickly. I tried to take a deep breath, but I couldn't feel any air sucking in through my mouth.

"Okay, I can do this. I know I can do this."

I moved my right hand to my chest. I didn't feel anything solid. In fact, I think my hand went straight through. I wanted to cry, but I couldn't. I couldn't even blink my eyes, I felt my eyelids drop down, but everything was crystal clear as if they were wide open.

"What am I going to do?"

I eyed the library door—it wasn't that far away. Maybe I just needed to focus on getting there. Slow and steady, I put one foot in front of the other even though they weren't touching anything solid. One by one, I moved my feet forward. It worked. The library door was closer.

"Hmm, I wonder if you don't need to move," I said to my feet.

I stretched out my arms and propelled my body forward. Just like that, I was flying, like a superhero, toward the door, and then through it. Not gonna lie, it was actually kind of fun and I felt like I accomplished something. This would have been so awesome if it didn't mean I was dead.

There was no one in the library, not even the librarian. A knapsack and a half-eaten fried chicken sandwich on a cafeteria tray sat on one of the rectangular tables. No doubt the school was evacuated after Kurt—did what he did. I was hoping to find at least one presence here. She wasn't alive either, but this was where she liked to hang out.

"Jessica! Are you here? We need to talk, like, right now!" I looked all around the library, hoping to see her. "I think I'm a ghost now, too."

I saw her watch me die. Wow, she was so upset. I really hoped that didn't mean she went to hell or something since she was the last one to give me advice to stand up to Kurt. That didn't make much sense, but I didn't know how any of this worked.

The sandwich on the table looked good, although I couldn't smell it. I never ate lunch today; maybe I needed to eat something to help clear my head. I grabbed for what was left of what looked like avocado with the chicken. My hand passed through it, and the table. That meant I couldn't eat anything. I looked down at my stomach realizing that I wasn't the slightest bit hungry or thirsty. Man, I had so many questions I needed to ask. Where was Jessica?

I waited as long as I could, but my friend never showed up. Wait, she said something about not being able to see other ghosts. Was that the case with me as well? That would be really bad. It meant we could pass each other a million times and never even know. Whoa, I could pass a whole bunch of ghosts and never know it. I thought about calling to her again, but I didn't see any point in it.

This was the absolute worst situation, and I had to figure it all out myself. How long would I be a ghost? Jessica did say something about that expert from a bunch of years ago saying ghosts had to figure out what they need to do to pass on. But if that was right, I had no idea whatsoever. It also didn't help knowing that, in about a hundred years, Jessica never figured it out for herself, either.

I lowered myself through the first floor and into a classroom. I floated to the window where I could see dozens of students spread out along the school's grounds. On a bench just a few feet from the window, Paige had her arm around Britney's shoulders. They were joined by a boy with long blond hair wearing a tank-top and baggy jeans. It was Todd Sullivan, Paige's sort of on-again, off-again boyfriend. He paced back and forth in front of the bench. Even with the girls' backs to me, I heard Britney sobbing.

"God, this sucks so much," she cried to Paige. "Why are they doing this to Kurt?"

"Brit, Kurt killed Sam," Paige answered. "We saw him do it. Kurt's eyes looked so psycho scary, then—"

"Kurt is not a psycho!" Britney pulled away from Paige, sliding across the bench. "They're going to lock him up, you know."

Todd stopped his pacing and faced the girls. "Maybe they should. I've never seen no one flip out like he did. I mean, he's snapped a few times on the football field, but not the way he did in the hallway with that skinny little twerp—"

"Shut up, Todd," Britney snapped. "You know Kurt. You know he's not like that. Now his life is probably ruined. It's so unfair."

"Unfair?" I shouted at the top of my lungs. "*He killed me!*"

Paige jumped up from the bench and faced the window. For a moment, I thought she was looking right at me.

Todd placed a hand on her shoulder. "Yo, Paige, are you all right?"

"I don't know, I thought I heard something." Her face squished with confusion. "It sounded like a voice, or maybe an echo. But I couldn't make out what it said."

"I think you're hearing things, Babe."

Britney slammed her fists against the bench. "This just sucks! Kurt's mom is going to be so upset."

My jaw dropped. It suddenly hit me. "*Mom!*"

Someone must have told her by now what happened. She must know I was killed today in school. I tried to push myself through the window, but some sort of force pushed me back. Another attempt caused the same result. I couldn't stay here. I needed to get home and see Mom. I couldn't believe I hadn't thought of her until now.

I backed up moving away from the window. Then I flew forward with as much speed as I could. This time, I bounced and ended up back where I started. The momentum knocked me upside down. With focus, I was able to spin around, but I still couldn't get past that window. Who would have thought glass would be a ghost's weakness? Somehow, I had to get home. Which meant I had to get out of this school.

"The front door!"

I flew as fast I could through the classroom door,

into the hallway, and into the school's lobby. Across from the safety officer's circular desk, the double doors leading to the outside were open. Lucky break since I don't think I would be able to open them myself. I hovered to it, ready to get home quickly and check on Mom. But, as soon as I hit the outside, I bounced back as if I ran into a solid wall. I approached again, trying to slowly put my right hand through. It jerked back. The problem wasn't the window's glass. It was the outdoors itself. Oh, no.

"I can't leave. I'm stuck in here," I realized. "Now what am I supposed to do?"

I wanted to cry so much, but couldn't. My eyes wouldn't tear up; my nose wouldn't run. I put my hand over my face but couldn't feel anything. That's because I was dead. Gone. Except I wasn't gone; I was still here. Yeah, I was no longer alive. My mother, however, was. She'd cry a river all over our kitchen floor once she found out I wasn't coming home, not today, not ever. I couldn't see her again, and she'd never see me.

"Oh, Mom," I sobbed. "I'm so sorry. Please forgive me."

I reached for the open doorway, but my hand bounced back again. I was stuck inside the school. But, for how long? How long would I be trapped in the one place I didn't ever want to be? How long would I have to call it…home?

Chapter Seven

I wasn't sure how many days went by—maybe a couple? It was hard to tell when every moment was exactly the same. The sun went down a few times, but I lost track. I searched the entire school for Jessica, even though I had a hunch I wouldn't find her. But I had to try, anyway. Turned out my hunch was right. I guess I was on my own.

The building had been empty for the last couple of days. In my confusion, I thought it meant I stopped seeing living people. Well, that wasn't completely true, I didn't see any living people except the safety officer who roamed the hallways and hung around the circular desk in the lobby until it was time for him to go home. It was a while before it hit me. I died on a Friday, and after that came the weekend. That was why no one else was in the building. But Monday morning had arrived, and the cafeteria was full of students chatting away at breakfast.

Everyone was divided up in their usual groups, having the same conversations while eating the same dry pancakes the kitchen served every Monday morning. Everything was back to normal as if I hadn't been killed in the middle of the hallway in front most of them just a few days ago. The fact that no one noticed me passing by was also normal, except last week I wasn't a ghost they couldn't see or hear. At that point,

44

people ignored me because I wasn't cool enough to be included in their groups.

As normal as things were here, I had a feeling it wasn't the case back home. My mom sure wasn't laughing over breakfast then going on with her day. I never even had the chance to say goodbye to her or let her know that I was okay. With almost two hundred students in the cafeteria, there had to be someone here who could see me. If I could find that person, I could send them to my home with a message for my mom. I could let her know not to worry about me, that I was okay.

I flew as high as I could without passing through the ceiling. All I could see were those circular tables and the tops of heads surrounding them. No one was looking up at me. At least not yet. I needed to change that, and fast. I didn't want to scare anyone, but right now, there was no other choice.

"Excuse me, Pinedale High!" It was as thunderous as I had ever shouted before. I waved my hands, trying to get someone's—anyone's—attention. *"Can any of you see or hear me? If you can, I really need to talk to you! I need a huge favor!"*

No one looked up. I wasn't too surprised considering how deafening the cafeteria was whenever the entire student body was in there. I could have been up here naked, and no one would have noticed. I tried one more time. *"Hello? Can anyone hear me? Ollie ollie, oxen free?"* Nope, still nothing.

I lowered myself to the floor next to a table of four boys who sat around one of the middle circular tables. They had playing cards in their hands. There were three cards with hearts in the middle of the table. One boy threw a queen of spades onto the table, then snagged all four cards and placed them in a pile next to a few more. He then tossed an ace of spades in the middle of the table, a move that made the boy across from him cheer while the other two cringed.

I had no idea what game these four were playing, but I did notice the stack of dollar bills sticking out of an unfolded napkin in front of one of them. From the designer collared shirts all four guys were wearing, which couldn't have come from Sullivan's, they were from the coffeehouse side of town. I stepped through the table so my upper body would stick out from the center where the cards were being thrown.

"Hey, can any of you hear me? It's Sam, the kid who was just killed last Friday?" I looked back and forth, but none of them took their eyes off the cards fanned out in their hands.

This was a waste of time. I left their game and peeked around the cafeteria for someone who might be able to see me. After a quick lap from one side to the other with no luck, a chuckle popped out from my throat. Except for the times Kurt was harassing and humiliating me, I always felt invisible in this school. People my age who knew me from town never even acknowledged me when I passed them in the school's hallways. It was like I had plenty of practice being a ghost.

I felt a tingle of excitement when Paige walked into the cafeteria with slumped shoulders. Whatever upset her, which I hoped was my death and not Kurt's arrest, didn't keep her from dying her hair over the weekend a darker red than it was on Friday. Her new shade matched her tiny pocketbook which looked brand new, and still had a tag on it. Even her shoes looked new and matched the color motif. No knapsack; Paige wasn't the type who brought books to school with her.

She may have heard me when I screamed through the window. I shouted her name and flew across the cafeteria, heading straight for her. Her head lifted as soon as I was in front of her. There was little reaction on her face. I couldn't tell if she was looking at me or across the cafeteria for someone else.

"Yo, Paige!" a female voice shouted from behind before I could say her name again.

Paige twirled around in time for Holly, another member of the coffeehouse clique, to clutch her hands and look her in the eyes. "Hey, babe!" Holly's green blouse looked pricey and brand new. So did the blonde dye job on top of her head. "I'm hearing some serious rumblings about Britney. Is it true?"

Paige sighed. "Yeah, it is totally true. She called me this weekend. Her parents enrolled her at a private school in Raleigh. Can you believe that bull-crap? She's not coming back here ever again."

"Wow, is that over what happened to Kurt last week?"

"Duh." Paige threw Holly an annoyed glance. "I tried calling you this weekend to tell you, but you weren't home."

"Saturday I was in Durham visiting some of my old friends." Holly put a hand on Paige's shoulder and smiled at her. "Let's go. I got something that'll make you feel a whole lot better."

Paige's head tilted. Holly held her pocketbook between them and popped it open. I flew over their heads so I could see what she was showing Paige. At first, I thought I saw a bunch of cigarettes held together with a rubber band. But, with a closer look, they were definitely not cigarettes. The edges were thin and each one looked like paper wrapped tight.

"I picked these up from some of those old friends." Holly slammed her pocketbook shut. "How about we go to our office and relieve some stress?"

Paige's face lit up like a headlight. "Yeah, let's do it."

A heavyset and balding man in a wrinkled polyester gray suit stomped through the cafeteria doors. A whistle hung from a black string around his neck. It was the school's assistant principal, Mr. Tuttle. I didn't know him well as we'd never spoken even once. His job was more about…honestly, I was never sure what he did in the school. This was the first time I had seen him in the cafeteria. For that matter, I don't remember seeing him roaming the hallways, like, ever.

Tuttle blew his whistle. The high-pitched shriek lasted about ten seconds. I tried to cover my ears but couldn't feel them. My hands passed through my head, and then through each other. The noise level in the cafeteria dropped in response.

"May I have your attention, please?" he announced. "Let's all quiet down, immediately!"

A lot of "shh" sounds filled the cafeteria while Tuttle tapped his foot against the floor, waiting.

Holly seized Paige's hand. They ran past Tuttle and out of the cafeteria. I soared after them. Paige may have been my only hope. Wow, who would have thought Britney Labelle's best friend would be my only hope? The irony wasn't lost on me.

"Ladies and gentlemen, please listen up! On Friday

afternoon, an unfortunate tragedy took place in our school!"

I stopped mid-way toward the door and looked over my shoulder. Tuttle was talking about me.

Once the assistant principal had complete silence, he went on. "An altercation took place which led to the death of one of your fellow students. It was a tragic moment in our school's history, but if something good is to come out of this unfortunate situation, it is that you now all understand why we speak so adamantly about controlling your tempers and reaching out to a staff member you trust when you feel such anger boiling up inside. Let Kurt Baker's actions serve as a lesson to us all." Tuttle nodded, then paused for what I took to be dramatic effect.

"Grief counselors from the district will be in the building later today for those of you who feel the need to speak with a professional about the tragedy. Right now, I ask you all to please stand up and bow your heads for a moment of silence as a sign of respect to the deceased. After that, we may begin our day."

Damn, for a guy looking to pay respects, he never even mentioned my name. He mentioned Kurt's, though.

The scuttling of everyone standing filled the cafeteria. Tuttle dropped his head and shut his eyes. Some students did the same. A lot didn't, but at least they stayed quiet. There were nearly two hundred students in the cafeteria for breakfast, yet if a mouse squeaked, we'd all hear it loud and clear. This was so rare, and it was all for me.

After a few seconds of complete silence, one lone voice filled the room. It was a boy in the back who sang. "Dah, dah, dah, dah…dah daaaaah!"

About a dozen other students shouted *"Charge!"* The room filled with laughter and a few cheers. The same boy in the back shouted, "Go, Pythons!" More students joined in the cheering. The Pinedale Pythons was the name of the school's football team. They held a vote on the team's name and mascot early last year. I didn't vote since I had no plans on going to any of the games, anyway. Sports were never my thing. Neither were school events, especially after hours.

Tuttle's head lifted with a look of disdain across his face. His cheeks were red. Another blow into his whistle was followed by the vice principal screaming at the students. His shouting was drowned by the chatter that had broken out at each table.

I'd seen enough of my in-school memorial. I dashed through the closed doors and into the hallway, hoping there was still time to catch up with Paige. She wasn't anywhere in the empty hallway. She had to be somewhere, right?

The door with a picture of a stick figure with long hair—the girls' bathroom—was a few feet from the cafeteria, across from the room with a stick figure that was bald—the boys' bathroom. I'd bet everything, which wasn't much even before I died, that Paige and Holly were in the girls' room. I stared at the door unsure of what to do. I wanted to charge in there and speak to Paige, but it felt weird thinking about going into forbidden territory. What if one or both was using the toilet? What if someone else was? I may have been a ghost now, but I was still a boy and had manners. What would my mom tell me to do right now? Screw it. This was for her, anyway. Time to go where no man had gone before.

I sucked in a deep breath of nothing, then floated through the door and into the girls' privacy. While the boys' room had two urinals against the wall by the sink and one small toilet stall, this one had an extra stall that was much larger than the other. I don't know why I was so surprised there were no urinals in here since that actually made sense. While the door to the smaller stall was wide open, the larger stall's door was closed.

"Go ahead," I heard Holly say from behind the closed door. "Take a puff."

"You really think I should?" Paige giggled.

"I promise, this stuff is good. It'll mellow you out."

I couldn't just stand here and wait for them to finish. I pushed my upper body through the door. Both girls were on their knees on opposite sides of the toilet. Smoke rose from the joint between Holly's two fingers. With her free hand, she held out a lighter and lit the end of Paige's joint. She waved her hand as a signal for Paige to stop stalling.

"Okay, here goes nothing,"

Paige stared at the joint, then put her lips on the end and inhaled. I lunged forward. Paige blew out a mouthful of smoke through my face. Her eyes suddenly ballooned to the size of grapefruits. The shocked-wide eyes and wider mouth meant she could see me.

"Paige!" I shouted. "I need your help—"

Paige slid backward across the floor. A high-pitched scream exploded out of her throat.

"What is it?" Holly asked, through a laugh. Her eyes narrowed into slits. "This stuff shouldn't hit you that fast."

"Paige it's me, it's Sam!" I waved a hand as if to

say hello. "I need you to do me, like, a huge favor, okay?"

"Oh my God!"

She jumped to her feet. She unlatched the door and dashed across the bathroom like a track runner trying to set a new record. I flew after Paige, shouting her name. She yanked open the door and ran out. I wasted no time going after her.

By the time I phased through the wall, Paige was halfway down the hallway. She looked back with panic written all over her face. "Stay away from me!"

"Paige, wait!" I pleaded, then chased her into the stairwell. "I need your help. Please, it's important!"

Paige scaled the stairs from the basement to the first floor. I followed her, determined to catch her and get her to listen to me. At the top of the stairwell, she put her back against the emergency exit. It was a door every student knew not to go through except during fire drills. Paige leaned against that door.

"It wasn't real I must have imagined it." She was breathing so hard I thought she was about to have a heart attack or something. "No more drugs...no more..."

I went face-to-face with Paige but kept a few feet's worth of distance. "Paige, please, chill out a sec, okay?" I held my hands out. "I just need you to—"

She let out a scream that was higher pitched than the last one. Her hand reached behind her and grabbed the emergency exit's latch. She pulled the handle, then pushed the door wide open. She ran out as if she was being chased by a wild animal.

"Paige, no! Wait! *Please!*"

I chased after her, but once I hit the open doorway,

I bounced backward, almost going through the staircase. I recovered in time to see the door closing and Paige far from the school, still running. So much for her being my only hope. I had a feeling I wouldn't be able to talk to her again, even if she did come back.

I glided down the stairwell looking to regroup. It was time for Plan B. The first thing I needed to do was figure out what that plan should be. If I couldn't think of something, there was no telling how long I'd be stuck in Pinedale Central High School. Jessica had been here for around a hundred years. I didn't even want to be here until graduation.

Just my luck, I was stuck here, as a ghost, in Haunted High School.

Chapter Eight

Time passed. I wasn't sure how much, at least nine
or ten years. Maybe a few more or less? It didn't
matter, not when every day flowed into the next. After a
while, I stopped counting days, then years. All I did
know was that Paige, Todd, and all the students I
started with graduated a while ago. New students came
in, and then graduated, too. After a while, I stopped
going to the ceremonies since they were the same, and
all kind of boring.

So far, three more students since Paige were able to
see me, or at least as far as I knew it was three. Two did
what Paige did. They freaked out and ran away from
me. The third was high, like, all the time. He swore I
was a hallucination. At least we were able to have some
good conversations until he graduated, or maybe he was
kicked out, I didn't know. After that, I stopped even
trying to be seen. I just kept to myself, spending most
of my time watching everyone as if they were
characters in a never-ending television show.

The adults, just like Jessica said, never saw or
heard me, even when I called to them. A lot of them
came and went, too. I saw three or four different
principals since Bronson left the week after I became a
ghost. The adults changed, too. Well, all of them except
for the custodian, Hank. I still couldn't tell his age, but
he had to be really old by now. The only things that

stayed the same in this school were him and me. I was still here, realizing I wasn't going anywhere, and there was nothing I could do about it. Sometimes, I wondered if Hank ever felt the same—

"Come on, Rex, please stop!"

A huge boy with red hair and freckles sandwiched a much smaller and skinnier boy between his huge frame and the wall. "I have to get to class," the small boy said through the wide eyes, behind his full rimmed glasses that looked too big for his face.

"No problem, Mikey." Rex held out his palm. "But there's a fee for walking my hallway, remember? There's also an additional fee for whining."

"I-I don't have any money." Mikey's voice shook.

"Then, what are we going to do about that?"

Rex took two handfuls of Mikey's shirt and lifted him off the ground. Mikey's glasses fell from his face and landed on the floor. This brought back memories for me, ones I really wanted to leave in the past. But I couldn't. I never forgot that coldness in my throat every time my bully tracked me down. The look on Mikey's face said he had that as well. Granted, he wasn't being lifted by his underwear like I was, and my bully never demanded money out of me. I guess we were about even. Well, at least until mine murdered me in the hallway.

While others kept walking, a group of five boys looked on, giggling. That was another thing that never changed. Bullying still went on in this school and others were entertained by it. The bigger, tougher kids still got their laughs from the masses at the expense of the smaller kids who weren't tough enough or strong enough to defend themselves. It was time for me, the ghost of Pinedale Central High School, to step in. I floated behind Rex and looked down at him from the ceiling.

"Hey! Back off!" I shouted. "Get away from him!"

Of course, Rex couldn't hear me. Neither could anyone else. In all the time I tried this, it never worked. There was one time the victim heard me but couldn't see me. It freaked him out, which only made things worse. He insisted there was a ghost in the hallway. Everyone laughed at him even more.

The door at the end of the hallway, the one leading to the front lobby, swung open. A brand-new adult stepped through and eyed the situation. He marched, not walked, through the hallway. As he moved closer, it was clear the guy was huge. He had to be close to six feet tall. Rex peeked over—as did everyone else—then dropped Mikey who slid along the wall. Rex stepped away.

The new guy walked into Rex's personal space and looked down into his confused eyes. There were some massive muscles under that white dress shirt which looked like it was ready to rip off his body. The noise in the hallway muted as the two stared eye-to-eye for what felt like forever.

After several awkward moments, the adult barked in Rex's face, "Name and age."

"What?" Rex stepped back. The big guy closed the gap.

Mikey snatched his glasses from the floor, then ran behind Rex as if he wanted to use the bully for protection. Every student in the hallway had stopped to watch.

"*Name and age!*" The man spoke with a fierceness

I had never heard from a teacher before, or even a principal. This guy was definitely different than any adult I'd seen in this building.

"Um, Rex Sullivan." Rex looked the big guy up and down. His shoulders were slumped, his nasty grin long gone. "I'm sixteen."

He held out his hand as if he wanted Rex to shake it. "I'm Mr. Copeland, the new guidance counselor for this school." He never broke eye contact.

Rex's head tipped back. "*You're* the new counselor?"

"That's right, and I believe you're in need of a counseling session." He motioned a finger over Rex's shoulder. "My office, now."

The students in the hallway let out a collective "Ooh."

"Oh, um, nah, I'm good." Rex leaned his upper body back like he was trying to escape Copeland's breath. "Thanks anyway…Sir?"

Copeland's eyes narrowed. He leaned forward so his mouth was inches from Rex's face. I moved in so I could listen to what he was about to say.

"Follow me to my office," he whispered, "or I will drag you there by your feet in front of everybody."

From the chuckling, I was sure other students heard Copeland's threat as well. Rex looked back and forth, dumbfounded, and more than a little embarrassed. "You're not serious, are you?"

Copeland's lips stretched into a smile. "Try me," he said, rubbing his hands together.

Copeland marched past Rex. Students scurried out of his way. He peeked over his shoulder at Rex, who followed. The biggest grin in the hallway was across

Mikey's face. Well, maybe besides my own.

I phased through the wall into the office where Copeland stood to the side of the door, holding it open for Rex to enter. "Take a seat. Now."

The counselor waved his hand at the two wooden chairs in front of a desk that had nothing on it except a computer, sitting at the side. Copeland waltzed around the desk and dropped onto the black cushioned chair which faced Rex and the empty chair. I drifted to the corner so I could have a front-row view of what was about to happen.

"If you're the counselor," Rex said in a huff. "Aren't you supposed to be asking me about my feelings and stuff?"

Copeland leaned forward, showing Rex his snarl. "Is anyone asking that boy you held against the wall about his feelings, Rex?"

"Listen, Mister...whatever you said." Rex waved his hands. "We were playing around, ya know? It really wasn't all that—"

"Now that we've met, let me tell you a bit about myself." Copeland folded his hands across the desk. "As you know, I'm new to this job. Before I came to Pinedale, I was a special ops soldier for the United States military. I've been in the middle of enemy jungles getting hunted, expecting to be ambushed by enemies who wanted to torture or even kill me, and having to navigate those jungles day after day, scared for my life. Can you imagine what that must be like, Rex?"

Rex pushed his back against the chair. His head tilted. "Uhm, no?"

"It's a horrible existence, and all you want to do is

get to the end of each day, knowing the odds are against you making it out safe and sound."

"I'm sure it was horrible." Rex's eyes squinted with confusion.

"Now, imagine what it must be like to be a teenager your age and having to go through that in school." Copeland pointed across the desk. "Because of you."

"I told ya, Mr. Copeland, we were just foolin' around." Rex tried to pass off the same explanation. "Mikey and I, we're friends. It's a game we play."

"Oh, I see." Copeland sat back and dropped his head. "I didn't realize it's just a game."

I widened my eyes into large circles. Mr. Copeland struck me as a smart guy. There was no way he would just accept this lame excuse, would he?

Rex began to stand up, but stopped when Copeland raised a finger, then peeked over at his computer screen. He typed a few strokes with one hand. "Rex Sullivan. You wouldn't be related to Chloe Sullivan, the lady who runs Sullivan's Discount Clothing, would you?"

"Yeah, I am. That's my grandma." Rex's head titled. "Why?"

"As I learned when I first moved to Pinedale, your grandmother opened Sullivan's Discount Clothing as a way of helping her community. She purposely keeps her prices low, and has even given clothes away to people, particularly children and teens, from impoverished families. Is that true?"

"Yeah, she does all that." There wasn't much pride in Rex's response.

"Your parents, Todd and Paige Sullivan, work

there as well, continuing with your grandmother's great contribution to Pinedale, don't they?"

"Yeah?" Rex's forehead squished, forming squiggly lines that ran from one side to the other. Even I was wondering where Copeland was going with this.

Copeland straightened his back. "Now, could you imagine how they'd feel if they knew their son spent his days in school bullying and taking money from the very children they've dedicated their business, and their lives, to improving, Rex? To find out that while they're helping to build lives in Pinedale, you're tearing down those same lives. You're bullying these kids and demanding from them the money your family helps their family save to survive. I'm guessing they'd be horrified by this. What do you think?"

Copeland rose from his chair. He slammed his hands against the desk, causing a bang which caused Rex to press his back against the chair. Copeland leaned forward, across the desk, bringing himself face-to-face with Rex. "So, how about I take a walk over to Sullivan's Discount Clothing, ask to speak with Todd and Paige Sullivan, and let them know what the students at Pinedale High School, their primary customers, are dealing with thanks to their son?"

Copeland straightened his back and stared down at his student with fists against his hips. "How about I let Chloe Sullivan know about how she gives away clothes, just so her grandson can demand the money they save back from them? Do you think she'd be proud of you, Rex?"

"I don't...I don't...know—"

"You *don't*?" Copeland's head popped forward. His head tilted with feigned surprise "Would you care to find out?"

Wow, I really did like this guy. Every hole in Rex's face opened wide, probably at how well Copeland knew him and his family. In truth, the entire family profile was on the computer screen. I could just imagine how he would have dealt with Kurt. Maybe I wouldn't have been so scared to come to school every day. Maybe I wouldn't have been killed here.

Rex's cheeks turned as red as his hair. "You're…you're the counselor. You're not supposed to do none of that."

Copeland's left hand balled into a fist and slammed a second time into the top of the desk. Rex's body jolted.

"As I said before, I'm still new at this job," Copeland explained with a hint of sarcasm. "I'm not sure what my functions are, but I do believe keeping the students here safe from any and all threats is one of them. So, I'm thinking that is exactly what I will do. I'm betting they have no idea you do this. Just think about how proud your family will be when they find out."

Rex threw his hands up in surrender. He said through a trembling jaw, "Okay, okay, I get it, man. I-I get it."

There was something about watching a bully get put in his place that pleased me. I tried to clap, but my hands couldn't touch; they just passed through each other. Too bad because Copeland deserved the applause. At least I thought so. I raised my arms in the air at the victory just achieved over one of the horrors that happens in this school. And I got to see it firsthand.

"I hope you do get it," Copeland replied. "Because,

if not, we have a problem, and one we can't fix. However, I am sure I'll bump into your family somewhere in this small town. Perhaps when I shop for clothes in their store. You get me, Rex?" Without a word, Rex shook his head back and forth.

"Yes! Way to go, Mr. Copeland," I shouted with pride. "You're the *man*!"

Copeland spun my way. His hip bumped against the desk. His eyes shot toward the ceiling where I was floating. His jaw twitched.

"What the hell are *you*?" He was looking directly at me.

Chapter Nine

Copeland stared at me; the stunned expression on his face mirrored my own. His fists were clenched like he expected me to attack him or something. But I wasn't a threat; I was confused. No adult had ever seen me before. Jessica had told me that adults couldn't see ghosts. Yet, I had an adult, the school counselor, gawking right at me. I figured I'd better explain myself, and fast. I just hoped he could hear me as well.

"Hi, my name is Sam," I said, through a wide smile. "Were you really a special ops soldier? If you were, that is, like, the coolest thing I've ever heard. Was it really the way you described it?"

"Mister Copeland?" Rex's head swarmed back and forth, looking across the ceiling. He seemed more confused than I felt. "What are you looking at?"

"Rex, get out." Copeland's gaze stayed my way. "Go to class."

Rex jumped out of his seat. He backed away from the desk. "Is this some sort of Vietnam flashback or something?"

"Vietnam?" Copeland's eyebrows scrunched, although he never looked away from me. "How old do you think I am?"

"Um, I don't know. The Gulf? Some other war or something? Listen, you're not really going to talk to my folks, are you—"

Copeland waved his hand to the door. "Out, Rex. Now!"

"Sounds good to me."

Rex about-faced, pulled open the door, and ran out as if the room was about to explode. The door swung closed. Copeland's mouth moved as he stared at me without blinking, but no words came out. So, I spoke first. "You know, Rex is probably already telling everyone the new counselor is a crazy man who was talking to someone who wasn't there."

"He may not be wrong."

Copeland's upper body tilted. He was trying to see every angle of me. I twirled in mid-air so he could see my back as well as my front. My mouth stretched into a huge grin. "You can really see me. That's so awesome!"

"Yes…yes, I really can see you." Copeland eyed the door. "But he couldn't see you. He couldn't hear you. I can, but not him."

I lowered myself to face Copeland. "The cool kids never could, or the mean ones. Just a few loners. Rex is sort of both, right? Adults can't see me either. Well, that's what I thought, until you."

Copeland reached out and put a hand through my chest. He yanked it back as if it touched lava. His eyes dropped down to my sneakers which were inches from the floor. He wandered around me. His hand popped out of my chest. "I've hallucinated before," Copeland muttered. "But they were always just a glimpse out of the corner of my eye. And it was always either someone I had to execute, or a poor innocent bystander who was caught in the way. I thought I dealt with that years ago in therapy."

"Whoa, you were in therapy?" I was more surprised to hear that than I should have been. "And now you're a counselor? That's wild."

Copeland stopped in front of me and once again examined me up and down. "I'm pretty sure I never killed a young black boy, so why am I hallucinating you? And why now?"

"Whoa, hold on. You think I'm imaginary?" Wow, I actually felt a little offended. How could he think I wasn't real? Then again, I remember at first, I thought the same about Jess. I moved toward Copeland, who skipped a step back. He raised his hands in front of his face in a defensive stance. "I'm not make-believe. I'm really here. I promise."

The look on Copeland's face changed. He now studied me as if I was an interesting piece of art. His fists unclenched as he let out a deep exhale. After several heavy breaths, he finally spoke. "If you are real, I have a hell of a lot more questions. Sam, right?"

"Yup, Sam. That's my name." I pointed to myself. "I loved how you handled Rex Sullivan. He bullies kids here, like, all the time. I've seen it a lot, but maybe now he won't. You put him in his place like no one else has. Do you think it's because you were a special ops soldier? You're, like, different than the other adults I've seen in the school. How long ago were you special ops? What was that like?"

"You know, for a ghost, you talk an awful lot." Copeland's fast breathing had slowed to a normal pace. He dropped into his chair. "Do all ghosts chat so much?"

"I have no idea." I drifted to the front of his desk. "The only ghost I've ever seen, I saw when I was still alive."

"Which was how long ago?"

I shrugged. "It's been a few years. Maybe, like, ten or something? I'm not so sure."

"Really?" Copeland's eyebrows rose. "You said adults couldn't see you. Yet here we are having a conversation. Can you tell me why I can see you when others haven't?"

"I don't know. I'm a ghost, not a ghost expert." I couldn't help but smirk. I finally got what Jess meant by that.

"Okay, so you're not here to hurt me, or the school. At least I don't suspect that's what this is." Copeland folded his hands across the desk. He wasn't scared of me anymore. I was really happy about that. "So, why are you here, Sam? Why are you haunting Pinedale Central High School?"

"I...don't know why I'm here." I looked up at the ceiling then back at Copeland. "I can tell you what Jess told me—"

"Hold on. Jess? Who is Jess?"

"Jessica, the other ghost I told you about, the one I met when I was still alive."

"Were there a lot of ghosts here when you were alive?"

"Jess was the only one I ever saw." I shrugged. "Anyways, she said we're ghosts until we can figure out what we have to do to move on."

"I see." Copeland scratched his chin. "I'm sure you've given this a lot of thought. What do you think you have to do to move on?"

I stared at him, lost for an answer. Copeland gave me a look that reminded me of spoiled food. "You haven't given this any thought at all, have you, Sam?" he asked.

"Not really, no."

"And you say you've been haunting this school for years?"

"I'm not sure how long it's been, and I wouldn't say I'm haunting the school, but yeah."

"Then maybe that's why I can see you, Sam." Copeland rose from his chair. "We need to figure out together what you need to do to move on."

"That sounds good. How do we do that?" Amazing how Copeland went from scared of me because I was a ghost, to wanting to help me, also because I was a ghost. He really was amazing, probably too amazing for Pinedale, but at the moment, I was glad he was here.

"Let's start from the beginning." Copeland clasped his hands together. "How did you die, Sam?"

"Oh. Uh…" My jaw trembled. The memory of everything that happened that day was fading, but the rage in Kurt's green eyes…that I'll never forget. "It's a lot to talk about."

"I'm sure, but I think it would be helpful to—"

A rapid tapping on the door proved to be a perfect interruption. The door, which had been left slightly ajar, pushed open. Rex waltzed into the office, then straight through me, stopping at the desk.

"Mr. Copeland, sir," he said with a huge fake smile. "I don't think you should go to our store and upset my grandma. She's kind of old and has a really bad heart. How about if we just deal with my behavior inside the school? Maybe detention or something?"

Copeland folded his arms across his chest. "Are you cutting class right now, Rex?"

"Nah, I'm legal." Rex reached into his back pocket and pulled out a piece of paper folded in fours. "My hall pass, to come talk to the school counselor."

"Good. Then, instead of talking about how to punish your behavior toward your schoolmates—" Copeland motioned to the chairs in front of his desk. "—how about we discuss how that behavior can change moving forward?"

"Mr. Copeland, I'll come back later." I lowered myself through the floor while Copeland peeked over at me and nodded.

I ended up in the basement's cafeteria. It was just past the school's second lunchtime, so there were no students hanging around. Two adult workers, wearing aprons, were busy cleaning off the circular tables. The janitor, Hank, pushed a mop through the cafeteria, sopping up all the spilled milk on the floor. Based on one untouched tray, I knew they had beef patties for lunch.

I was kind of relieved by Rex showing up when he did. Copeland believed it would help to talk about what happened with Kurt, and maybe he was right. But I didn't feel ready to relive that experience. Maybe I should have, anyway. It sucked that soon this day would be over, everyone would leave the school, and I'd be stuck just roaming the hallways by myself with not too much to keep me busy. It was something I still wasn't used to by now, even if it was still boring.

But I did like talking to Copeland and I planned to stop by his office again in the morning, and maybe a lot of mornings after. A real special forces agent. How cool was that?

Chapter Ten

A few days or more went by and I chatted with Copeland a lot. I was in that office whenever he was free and not with a student, or at times, an adult who worked at the school. I even sometimes hung out in there at night when the school was empty. I felt safe in the counselor's office, which is something I could never say back when I was alive. I didn't even know the school counselor back then. So far, most of our talks focused on what it was like to be a ghost. We barely talked about my life before I died, but I had the feeling he was setting up to get into the harder stuff later.

"I guess being dead isn't the worst thing," I explained to Copeland who sat in his chair across the desk. "I do miss eating, sleeping, and even using the bathroom, but besides that—"

A knock on the door shook my attention. Mr. Copeland looked through me at the clear window in his office door. He waved a hand, telling me to chill for a second, then he stood up.

Copeland marched to the door and pulled it open. It was long-time teacher, then assistant principal, now the newest principal, Ms. Kouriki. At barely five feet, Kouriki looked like another student standing face-to-chest with Mr. Copeland. Then again, he was huge even for an adult. Everyone looked small next to him.

"How may I help you, Principal Kouriki?"

Copeland asked with confidence radiating from his tone. She eyed his right arm before looking up into his eyes. I'd seen her do that before. The tattoo of a sword with two arrows shooting through it showed under his white sleeve.

I stood against the desk...well, "stood" wasn't an accurate description. It was more like I hovered with my feet a few inches above the floor. I couldn't physically stand on the tile. If I tried, I'd end up going right through. Then I'd find myself back in the cafeteria again.

The two stared at one other for what felt like forever. I had seen lots of students, and even staff, flinch at the principal's stern and puffy scowl. But not Mr. Copeland. He never flinched even though he had only worked in the school for a few weeks or so. The guy was so different from anyone else I'd known. Maybe that's why he became the first adult who could see and hear me. Or it was coincidence; I really had no idea.

"Good afternoon, Mr. Copeland." Kouriki spoke like a colonel in the army addressing a soldier. "I have a parent in my office who is new to Pinedale. She is looking to tour the school for her son's enrolment. I would like to pass this on to you."

"It's not a good time," Copeland answered. "I'm conducting a session."

Kouriki's gaze fell onto the office. I waved hello while watching her narrowed eyes through my transparent hand. "I don't see anyone else in here," she growled. "Do you, Mr. Copeland?"

The counselor grinned. "What I mean is I have a scheduled session about to start. The student is on his way."

Kouriki responded with a sigh. "Very well. I will get someone else. But, please keep in mind, as a guidance counselor for Pinedale Central High School, conducting tours does fall under your job requirements."

"I do understand that." Copeland threw her a thumbs-up. The principal about-faced and journeyed down the hall. Copeland shut the door then returned to his chair behind the desk. I hovered in front of him, keeping myself straight as best as I could.

"Man, that lady is so uptight, like, all the time." I let out a snort. "So, where were we?"

"As I recall, Sam…" Copeland leaned forward. "You were about to tell me how you lost your life."

"Oh, that again." I let my smile fade. I really did hate this topic, and I was pretty sure that wasn't what we were just talking about. In fact, I don't believe Copeland had asked me about that except for the first time we met. I guess he was trying to be slick. Or he felt it was time to start getting into the hard topics.

"Let's start with something easier." The counselor's hands folded across the desk. "Instead of telling how, can you tell me when you lost your life? Do you know the year it happened?"

"Um…" Yup, we were done talking about the easy stuff. I gave his question some thought. For as long as it had been, I couldn't remember the exact date. Sure, there were a lot of calendars around the school, but I floated by them, never paying attention. Heck, I barely paid attention to dates when I was alive. "I know it was…a while ago."

"Yes, I presumed that was the case." His gaze rose

to the top of my head. "I also assumed it was a lot longer than you estimated when we first spoke. The Jeri curl has been out of style for a long time. I think with the kids today, it's all about dreads."

I reached for the top of my head. It was an instinctive move since it wasn't like I could actually touch it. "Mom couldn't afford to take me to the barber, so she did my hair herself." I shrugged. "What can I say? She liked Jeri curls."

"My apologies. I didn't mean to make you feel insecure."

"No biggie. I'm good." I crossed my legs in mid-air and smiled. "Hey, can we talk about you some more? Were you, like, really a secret agent for the government? Like, with missions and stuff? That is soooo cool."

"Special forces unit, yes," Copeland answered through a slight grin. "And I wouldn't call it 'cool.' It was dangerous, and necessary."

It sure sounded cool to me. "How long did you do that?"

"I enlisted at a young age and moved up quick. I retired a few years ago, then resumed my education to become a school counselor. That's what brought me here."

"So, you're not from Pinedale, are you?" I'm not sure why I asked, I already knew the answer. Nothing about Mr. Copeland screamed "small town guy." But he was the first person I had met who wasn't from Pinedale.

"Not at all." Copeland shook his head and grinned. "I'm a Brooklynite, born and raised."

"Brooklyn, like New York City?"

"Yes, like New York City."

"Wow. Why did you come here?"

"Retirement from service led to a need to go somewhere." He shrugged. "I guess I wanted a change of lifestyle. Something different than the big city where I grew up. I definitely found that here in Pinedale." He gazed at the ceiling. "There is a certain charm to walking into the stores where I know the workers, and they greet me by name."

That sure sounded boring to me, just like Pinedale. Why he'd give up the big city for a town that's surrounded by farms and cornfields didn't make sense. Then again, half of Pinedale was made up of families whose grandparents and great-grandparents moved here from all over the country, so maybe there was something to it. My goal was to leave and get as far away from Pinedale as I could. I guess that didn't work out too well.

"But, before you retired, you did take down bad guys, right?" I leaned my elbows against the desk. Well, not really. I just kind of leaned them against the air above the desk. "Like, can you seriously kick ass the way they do in the movies?"

My question made him chuckle. "Nothing like the movies, Sam." Copeland straightened his back and stared down at my widened eyes. "But the short answer is yes. I was trained for combat along with the rest of my SEAL team. However, my specific expertise was in behavioral psychology."

"Behavioral…what does that mean?"

The counselor's grin grew into a full-fledged smirk. "It means I'm trained to read people's subtle cues." He scratched the bottom of his chin. "Like how you have changed the subject, and you're flattering me in order to avoid my question."

"Ooh, you caught that, huh?" If my face could turn red, it would have. I thought I was being slick, but the guy saw right through me. And I didn't mean because I was a ghost. "I-I don't think I like to talk about it. You get that, right?"

"I do. Perhaps talking about it would help, though."

"Help?" I raised my eyebrows. "How would talking about it help?"

"For starters—" Copeland cupped his hands together across the table. "—last week, you told me your goal was to figure out the reason you're still here. Why haven't you passed on? Why are you still a ghost after all this time?"

Hmm, another topic I forgot I agreed to discuss. But that was because I wasn't sure what to say. Why was I still a ghost after all this time? Why was Jessica a ghost after an even longer time? Nothing about it made sense to me, and it wasn't like I had anyone who did know to talk to about it. Even Jessica barely understood the "rules" of being a ghost, and, at the time, I didn't have a reason to pick her brain on that subject. Now that I did need her advice, I hadn't even seen or heard from her—or any other ghost—since my death.

"I guess I don't know," I answered.

"To find that answer, I think it best we talk about the day you died and became a ghost in the first place."

Maybe Copeland did have a point. I spent a lot of time avoiding the subject with myself, or the few people I could talk to over the years. That was because my brain wanted to explode every time the memory of that day popped in there. It wasn't a cool moment for me. But here I was still floating around, not even close to moving onto wherever dead people went. Perhaps it was time to talk about it, especially with Mr. Copeland—

Another knock on the door shook me from my thoughts. Copeland stood, walked around his desk, and opened the door. A girl with dyed pink hair and a huge nose ring stormed in with clenched fists. She dropped onto one of the two chairs in front of the counselor's desk and growled like an angry wolverine.

"What's going on, Kaela?" Copeland asked, with a hint of levity.

"I swear to God, I'm going to throw fists with Ms. Keening," she snarled. "It's gonna happen. Just watch!"

Man, Ms. Keening's mom was a teacher here back when I was a student. Everyone hated her class, even the good kids. Screaming at students over stupid stuff was her favorite thing to do. After peeking into this Ms. Keening's classroom many times, I could say for sure that they were no different from each other. She screamed just as much, maybe even more, than her mom did.

In fact, the only difference was this one had light brown hair while the old Mrs. Keening's hair was gray. This one frightened me just as much as the last one, even though she couldn't see or hear me. I wasn't surprised at all that most of the students who barged into Copeland's office were pissed off at her.

Copeland threw me a glance. "We'll talk later," he said, under his breath.

"No, I need to talk now!" Kaela shouted.

"Right, that's what I meant. Let's talk now."

"My God, you're so weird," Kaela moaned.

Copeland nodded my way, then sat next to Kaela, placing a hand on her shoulder to help calm her down. I passed through the wall into the hallway, floated down to the cafeteria, then into the school's gym on the same floor. I liked watching the classes play basketball. Despite being smaller than almost everybody else, basketball was a sport I was really into back when I could still touch the ball. I couldn't shoot too well, but I was fast enough to play good defense. Well, maybe "good" was a stretch, but I had fun. It was something from my life I missed. A lot.

On some nights, I pretended to play and get the winning shot at the buzzer. I'd raise my arms and then do a victory dance, pretending I could hear the crowd's cheers. Of course, it's not as much fun without an actual basketball in my hands, or people to pass back and forth. Ah well, maybe next life.

Chapter Eleven

It was another long night of swimming through the hallway and pretending to win the gold medal in the Olympics. After a while, I noticed the sun rising through the windows. Morning had finally arrived. I never looked forward to mornings back when I was alive because it meant having to walk into this school. Part of each day was spent navigating the hallways past my bully. Not that a lot of the students besides him were good-hearted people—too many followed the bullies. There were some kind and caring students, but they were outnumbered by the heartless jerks and their followers by about three to one.

Now that I was a ghost, I liked the crowded hallways during the weekdays. There were still plenty of bullies, like Rex, in the school now, but they weren't as violent or as relentless. Also, watching the students and adults scurry around helped make the time fly by. Even the weekends still had a security guard sitting at that circular desk in the lobby watching TV on his phone. I liked hovering over his shoulder and staring at the screen, even if most of the shows were in Spanish and involved couples either arguing with each other or making out.

It wasn't long before Mr. Copeland wandered through the hallway and entered his office. He was always the second person to arrive after the school's custodian, Hank. I entered Copeland's office to see him at his desk with a bagel and coffee, as was his normal routine. I floated near the floor and snuck behind him while he opened his newspaper.

I waited for Copeland to swallow a mouthful of coffee then brought my face close to his left ear. I screamed as loud as I could, "Boo!" I also stretched my face into what I guessed had to look scary.

"Good morning, Sam." Copeland never even looked up from his newspaper. It was hard to believe that not long ago, the man nearly jumped onto the desk after seeing me for the first time. To his credit, he calmed down fast, took a deep breath, and then spoke to me as if I was one of his students. After that, he always acted like seeing me was no big deal. Maybe to him, it wasn't. He'd seen some rough stuff in his life.

"Damn. One day, I'm going to surprise you."

"You haven't yet." Copeland finally lifted his head and looked my way. "But you're always welcome to try, Mr. Anderson."

My head snapped back. I was sure I'd never told him my last name. "How do you know?" In all honesty, it had been so long since I heard the name said by anyone, including myself. I almost forgot what it was.

Copeland closed his newspaper and folded it in half. He dropped it on the desk, reached into the top drawer, and pulled out a beige folder. "What is that?" I asked, guessing it had something to do with me.

"Over the last few nights, I've been online researching student deaths that happened in this school throughout its history." Copeland looked at me with widened eyes. "I was taken aback by how many there had been over the years, including adults. I found articles on two separate fires in this building. One was in the early twentieth century, the other was in the 1950s. Both led to the deaths of several students and staff."

"Fire? Really?" I vaguely remembered Jessica mentioning she died in a huge fire.

"There was a lot to go through, but I found some of the answers I was looking for on one particular case."

"You mean me, right?"

"I do."

I leaned in close, curious what Copeland had found out about me. He placed a newspaper article printed on white computer paper on the desk. Above four lines of text, it had my junior high school graduation picture, a picture I had taken a year and a half before I became a ghost. Wow, I was actually in the newspapers as if I was someone famous. Not that I wanted to be famous for dying in school, but at least my picture was in print and would last forever.

"This article is from twenty-eight years ago, Sam," Copeland explained. "According to this, you lost your life in a physical altercation with another student named Kurt Baker."

"*Twenty-eight years*?"

My ghostly body darted back. I nearly lost control of myself. I couldn't believe what he had just said. But it did make sense considering how much change I'd seen here.

I shook my head as the realization hit. "Twenty-eight years. I guess so, yeah."

Wow, I never realized how long I'd been floating around the school. To me, it could have been, like, a few years, a decade at the most. Then again, it could have also been a hundred years. Since that day, time went both fast and slow at the same time.

"What else does it say about me?"

"That's pretty much it. Not a lot of details." Copeland let the paper slip from his hands. "I'm betting there's more to this story, isn't there?"

"A lot more." The words shot out of my mouth before I thought better of it. This guidance counselor was slick. He had me talking even though I made it clear I didn't want to touch the subject. Maybe, deep down, I did want to talk about it, and it was easy to talk to Copeland. Fine, here goes...

"Kurt was the biggest freshman here at Pinedale High, and I was the smallest. I guess that's why he picked me on day one. I wish I didn't have to be stuck here with him. But Pinedale only has one high school, so there was nowhere else to go. Each day, he got a lot worse with the wedgies, the shoves, and the comments whenever he passed me in the hallway. Would you believe Kurt would sneak up on me and yank me off the floor by my underwear? He did that in our first week, and then almost every day since. The guy had the whole school laughing at me and looking at me like I was dog crap. It happened all the time."

"That sounds rough for you, Sam. I'm sorry. I truly am." Copeland tapped the article resting on his desk. "What happened on that day?"

"My second year here, nothing changed. Everyone kept telling me to stand up to him. My mom said it, the principal, and the other kids said it. Hell, even Jessica, that ghost I told you about, said it. So, I finally did."

I held a hand in front of my face and made a fist. "I finished lunch and was heading back to class when I felt Kurt running up from behind me and going for my underwear. This time, I spun around and hit him as hard as I could in the stomach. It stopped him in his tracks and knocked him off his feet. Now, everyone in the hallway was laughing at Kurt and cheering me. It was the greatest moment of my life."

Copeland nodded his approval. His smile faded. "Finish the story, Sam."

My gaze dropped to the desktop. This was the part I didn't like thinking about, let alone saying it out loud. "Kurt's face, it turned all red. I saw this anger in his eyes, like he turned into a demon or something. He slammed me against the wall and wrapped his hands around my throat. I think something just snapped in him. I couldn't breathe and he didn't care."

A tear rolled down Copeland's cheek. I tried to cover my face with my left arm, but that didn't help. We could still see each other clearly. To think, after all this time…almost thirty years…I still hadn't gotten completely used to the whole being a ghost thing.

Copeland wiped the back of his hand across his face. He inhaled and straightened his back. "Please, go on."

"I heard everyone cheering, then they were freaking out, screaming. Some of the students tried to pull him off me, but he wouldn't let go, not even when the adults yanked on his arms, yelling at him to stop. The next thing I remember is floating near the ceiling and looking down at my body until they covered me with a blanket. I also saw police officers walking through the double doors to the front desk with Kurt. They had him in handcuffs. The funny thing is, the whole time, I didn't struggle. I just kept waiting for him to let me go. I never thought he'd choke me until I died. But that's exactly what he did."

"And you've been haunting this school ever since."

"Haunting?" I chuckled. "Yeah, I guess I have been haunting the school. I'm the ghost of Pinedale Central High School." I raised my hands and wiggled my fingers. "Wooooo!"

"Well, every student needs a path."

I did a doubletake. Did Copeland just make a joke? There wasn't even a grin across his face to show it, but that definitely sounded like he was trying to be funny. It made me want to talk more. Maybe that was why he said it.

"Hey, you want to know the worst part, Mr. Copeland?" I paused. Copeland motioned me to answer. "For years, I heard the teachers all talking about it. After a while, they'd call Kurt by his name, but I was 'that kid.' None of them remembered anything about me except that I got killed by Kurt Baker in the hallway."

Copeland's knuckles rapped against the desk. "That must have been difficult for you to hear."

"It was," I answered. "I heard Kurt went to juvie, but he was let out when he turned eighteen. That means he was only locked up for two years. Can you believe that? Taking my life was only worth two lousy years."

"That's not entirely the case." Copeland pulled another sheet of paper from the folder and held it in front of his face to read. "I found a few articles on Kurt Baker from newspapers. According to one, after his release, he tried to return to this school to finish his education. He was rejected."

"Lucky for everyone here." I rolled my eyes.

"I found an appeal he put in with the district at the age of nineteen, but they turned him down as well." Copeland lowered the paper so I could see his face. "He went onto fail the high school equivalency exam twice. Not long after, he was arrested and convicted on two charges of burglary and one charge of attempted manslaughter."

"So, he went back to jail?"

I didn't mean to sound so excited about that, but I sure wasn't sorry to hear it. Copeland nodded. I tried to hold in my emotions over the news, but I couldn't help but laugh. "Well, that'll make my floating around here forever a little easier."

"It doesn't have to be forever, Sam." Copeland stood up. As always, my eyes wandered to the stomach muscles showing through his white shirt. There was definitely a solid six-pack underneath that expensive collared shirt. "As we've discussed in the past, you just have to figure out what is keeping you here on this plane of existence."

"As we've discussed?"

"More specifically, as I've tried to discuss but you've avoided." Copeland clapped his hands. The slap echoed throughout the room. "Maybe it's time we stop avoiding that conversation and tackle it head-on. Let's figure out what it would take for you to move onto the next plane of existence."

"You really believe in that stuff, Mr. Copeland?"

He let out a snort. "You know what? I was never too sure before, but now…" Copeland waved his hands my way. "I still think there's a small chance I'm hallucinating you. But if not, I need to seriously rethink my beliefs on life after death."

"Gotcha." I rose to the ceiling with my hands high above my head. They went straight through the plaster. "I'll see you again tomorrow, Mr. Copeland. Thanks for looking all that up."

"It's my pleasure, Sam." I was about to say goodbye and let him get back to his work. Copeland raised a hand before I could speak. "Hold on, one more thing."

"What's up, Mr. Copeland?" I glided down from the ceiling.

"I was reluctant to share this, but I think you should know I looked up your mother last night on my computer."

"My mom?" My head picked up. "You did? Really?"

Copeland waved his hand as a signal for me to come closer to his desk, which I did as quickly as possible.

"To be honest, I couldn't find too much since the incident, but I did come across a few social media posts on her. She moved to Miami about twenty-two years ago."

"That makes sense. She always talked about wanting to be near family. I had a lot of cousins there. Is that all you found out?"

"No, there was something else." Copeland grinned. "My search led me to an exposé on Aisha Parker."

"Who is that?"

"Aisha Parker is one of three foster children who were raised by Ella Anderson."

"My mom?"

"Yes." Copeland slid the paper across the desk. "Aisha Parker grew up to become a lawyer specializing in teenage harassment cases."

The article had a black and white photo of Mom. She had wrinkles on her face and she wore glasses, but it was her with an arm around a pretty and petite woman I guessed was Aisha Parker. Wow, I guess Mom found someone who needed her love after I died. She raised kids in need of a family, probably to make up for losing me. I was happy to hear that. If only I could tell her that.

"Ooh!" A sudden burst of excitement made me gasp. "Mr. Copeland, let's call her. I wanted, like, forever to let her know I'm okay, and that I love her."

"That's a really bad idea, Sam."

I gasped again. This time the excitement dripped out of me like helium from a leaky balloon. "Why is it a bad idea? I think it's a great idea. She'd want to know I'm okay, don't you think? I need her to know I'm okay!"

"You're not okay, Sam. You're dead."

"I know I'm dead, but…but…"

Copeland let out a sad sigh. I wanted to be so angry, but I knew his deep exhale was out of sympathy for me. He was the only friend I had, so I had to keep my cool.

I faked a deep breath. Even though I couldn't actually suck in any air, I wanted to show him that I was calm and mature. "Mr. Copeland, why is it a bad idea for you to give a message to my mom?"

"What would you have me say to her, Sam?" He placed his left hand against the side of his face, in the shape of a telephone. "Good morning, Ms. Anderson, you have no idea who I am, but I'm in touch with the ghost of your long dead son. He wants to let you know he's just fine."

Copeland pulled his hand away from his face. "I'm sure she's spent plenty of the last twenty-eight years coping with your death. Believe me when I tell you, that phone call, whether she believes me or not—and I'm sure she wouldn't—would traumatize her all over again. Do you want to do that to her after all this time?"

I wanted to scream "yes" at the top of my lungs. Nothing was more important to me than hearing Mom's voice one more time, even if it was over the phone. I wanted to argue, beg, or force Copeland to pick up the phone and make that call. But, deep down, I knew he was right. Mom was an emotional type, especially when she was caught by surprise. I didn't know how old she was now, but I remembered her seeing doctors, like, all the time and saying something about her heart being weak. If she was doing well, I wouldn't want to cause a problem.

"Okay, no call. For Mom's sake." I turned toward the door. "I-I think I need to go."

I was about to zip through the door and into the hallway but was stopped by the sound of Copeland's voice calling out to me. "You're making the right decision, Sam, for her sake."

"I guess."

"And I do believe you will find a way to move on and be at peace. If you stop avoiding the subject, I'm sure of it."

"I haven't moved on yet, Mr. Copeland."

I changed directions and phased through the ceiling, into an empty classroom. I really wanted to be mad at Mr. Copeland for not calling my mom. But I liked him so much, I just couldn't stay upset. Plus, he made a good point…as always. Talking to Mom, hearing her cry over me, it wouldn't have been good for either of us. Not after almost thirty years. Also, speaking about the Kurt incident, even after all this time, did make me feel a little bit better.

I was sure I'd be back in his office soon enough. Maybe then, I'd bring up Kurt again and we could get into it a bit more. It wasn't like we had much else left to talk about, anyway. But Mom was one subject I knew I didn't want to talk about ever again. Let her live in peace.

Chapter Twelve

It turned out there was a lot more to talk about than just Kurt. A week passed and my "counseling sessions" with Copeland really heated up. We focused a lot on my feelings, both when I was alive and since I've been dead. Even though I didn't want to, and I swore I wouldn't, he got me to talk about my relationship with my mom.

I told him I understood why we couldn't call her. In response, Copeland told me he felt some guilt about shooting me down on that, or even telling me what he found out about her in the first place. I was glad he did, though. She was an old lady now, and she'd probably moved on with her life. Still, it bothered me that I'd never get to hear from her, and she'll never hear from me, ever again. That was a lot to accept, but I had to get over it for her sake.

Copeland gave me a lot to think about over the weekend. He made it sound like a homework assignment, and one that would take up a lot of time during those two long days. I did it because, really, what else could I do with my time?

It wasn't like I never tried to leave the school; I just couldn't. The walls, the doors, and the windows were like shields that knocked me back whenever I touched them. One time, I sailed across the entire building, picking up as much speed as I could. My body flew back as if I hit a cement wall at the other end. It was like being in a prison except I didn't do anything wrong.

Earlier in the week, Mr. Copeland wanted to see what happened when I tried to leave the school. He held open the front door and told me to try to go through. He did the same with the side door, a window, and even the doorway to the rooftop. At first, I thought he was getting a kick out of watching me bounce and flip in the air. But he insisted it was just a matter of trying everything possible before saying I couldn't do it. That made sense, I guess, but it wasn't like I hadn't tried before.

Three o'clock arrived. I looked out the window on the first floor as the school cleared out and the front yard filled with students heading home for the day. I kept an eye on one particular student. Rex Sullivan strolled past Mikey and a few of his "smaller" friends, never looking their way. Mr. Copeland was their hero, even if they'd never know it. Hopefully, that would last.

Speaking of Copeland, the light from his office shined from the thin space between his door and the floor. I peeked through the window on the door to see him in his chair staring at the computer screen. With a grin, I lowered myself through the floor so only my head was sticking out. I then phased through the door and slowly moved toward the desk. I felt like a shark sneaking up on its prey. This time, I was going to catch him completely by surpr—

"Hello, Sam."

Dammit. I floated up so my entire body was inside the office and in front of Copeland's desk. "It looks like everyone's gone home. Why are you still here?"

"Truth be told," Copeland lifted his head and looked my way. "I was waiting around for you."

"Really?"

"Yes, I knew you'd float in here eventually." Copeland folded his hands. "You do hang out in this office after I leave, right?"

I widened my eyes. "How do you know?"

"I suspected. Now I know for sure." He flashed me a slight smirk. "Anyway, I want to try something new, if you're interested. At this time, we're less likely to be interrupted."

"Okay, let's do it!"

Copeland grinned. "I didn't say what it is yet, Sam."

Of course, he was right. I had no idea what Copeland had in mind. Whatever it was, I was interested. In the time we had spent together, I found that I trusted this man one hundred percent. Hopefully it was something cool.

Copeland stopped moving and gave me a knowing stare. He was waiting for me to ask, so I did. "What is it you want to try?"

"I believe that, deep down, you know exactly why you can't move on. So, I'd like to speak with your subconscious, and bring the answer out of you."

"How do you do that?"

"Through hypnosis."

"Really?" I opened my eyes wide. "You know how to hypnotize people?"

"It was part of my training. I used the technique a few times on prisoners during my interrogation days." He looked at me with raised eyebrows. "Of course, in those cases, it involved drugging them up for the sake of cooperation, but I'm sure that won't be necessary here."

I tipped my head back. All I got out of that was something about drugging people up. "I don't understand. What are you going to do to me?"

"I'm going to attempt to relax you into a dream-like state. Once you're in that relaxation state, I will put you in touch with your subconscious. The conscious tends to have doubts, so it hides the answers that, deep down, we actually know." Copeland stood with an aura of determination. "What do you say, Sam? Would you like to give it a try?"

I nodded an excited "yes." There wasn't too much Copeland could have asked that I would have said "no" to. Besides, I'd never been hypnotized before, and I was curious. Although I did have one lingering question bouncing around in my head.

"Um, are you sure you can hypnotize a ghost?" I asked.

"Honestly, I have no idea." Copeland waltzed around the desk. "I'll need to modify some of the techniques, but how about we give it a try?"

"You mean, like, right now. Right?"

"Yes." Copeland waved a hand over the chair closest to him. "Have a seat, Sam."

I did my best to follow the instructions considering I couldn't actually sit on the chair. I placed my back and butt as close to the seat as I could without falling through the wood. I then held myself in place.

"Good." Copeland circled me. "Now, close your eyes."

"I can't close my eyes. If I do, I can see through my eyelids."

"That's a problem." Copeland stopped his circling, coming to rest on my left. "Okay, then. Let me try this in a different way. I'm going to attempt to use your body to take you into that state of pure relaxation."

I glanced up at him. "You know I don't have a body, right, Mr. Copeland?"

"It's a mental thing, Sam. Now, don't speak, just listen to the sound of my voice."

"Yes, sir." I didn't want to tick him off. Copeland really wanted to help me. And, in truth, he was the only friend I had. That was still one more than I had when I was alive.

Copeland wandered behind me. His fingers tapped the back of the chair. He leaned over me. "I got it."

"What have you got?"

"Sam, one thing I know you want is to be able to go outside, correct?"

My gaze focused on the window behind the desk. "Yeah. Very much. I haven't been outside in, what, almost thirty years—"

"Okay. I want you to look through that window, Sam, to the outside." Copeland's voice was a whisper inches from my left ear. "Clear your mind and concentrate on nothing except what is past that glass. See the grass on the ground. Look at every blade and see how they each blow in the wind."

I did exactly what he said, staring at the grass. I've watched it before through the window, but never at the single strands. They were farther from one another than I ever realized.

"Now, slowly lift your head to the sky. See the clear blue sky with the light shining from the sun. Now, look at the single cloud as it moves from one side to the other."

Copeland's voice slowly grew from the whisper. His hands passed through my shoulders and clamped on the back of the chair. From the distance between our faces, I'd probably be able to smell his aftershave lotion if I could smell anything.

"As you look at the sky, I want you to focus on the air around you. It flows through you, Sam, from all sides. You can feel it against your arms, against your knees, and against your back. It blows into your face."

This was really cool. At least for the moment, following his instructions, I was a bit lost in the sky. I thought I did feel air around me. It made my skin tingle. I wanted to ask Copeland if this was real, or my imagination. Then I remembered he told me not to speak. I don't think I wanted to know because I didn't want the experience to stop.

"Now, I want you to lower your head and focus on your feet, and on the white sneakers around them. Imagine them against the floor. How it touches the soles of your sneakers. Can you feel the floor against your feet, Sam?"

I nodded ever so slightly. For a moment, I thought I actually did touch the floor under my feet.

"Now, look up at the window, at the grass outside in the yard. Feel the chair against your body, along with its solidity. Now, sense yourself on the chair in the middle of that patch of grass. The temperature around your body is warm due to the sun high above. Imagine the heat on your face, arms, and legs. Remember how the sun felt against your skin when you were alive. It feels the same right now. Smell the fresh-mown grass. Hear the birds chirping in the far distance."

As I looked around, I could tell I was still in Copeland's office. Yet, I felt the fresh air in my face, the warmth against the top of my head. My feet touched something solid. I thought it was the floor, but it seemed much softer. Grass. There was grass under my sneakers. I tried to sit up straight. That's when I realized I was sitting, not floating. The chair rubbed against my back, or at least I sensed the wood. Holy cow! I reached up with my left hand. It touched something—someone's knuckles, maybe? Whatever it was, my fingers actually made contact, or at least it seemed that way.

Copeland made a sound. It may have been a gulp. Was that real? I knew none of this could be real, yet I heard the wind howling, and smelled the fresh-cut lawn odor in the air. I heard chirping. Only my eyes told me it wasn't real. When I looked up and squinted, it was still the ceiling in the office. Copeland's desk was still in front of me, and the outside was on the other side of that window—

A body passed through the office. I caught it out of the corner of my right eye. Someone—another ghost—stopped in mid-float and looked my way. I swung my head over. Whoever it was—a guy, I think—was gone. Was he real, or my imagination caused by this hypnosis stuff?

"Sam, can you still hear the sound of my voice?"

"Yeah, I can…"

Someone else floated in front of the window. Even though I hadn't seen her in a long time, I remembered the long hair and old-fashioned dress as if I had seen them yesterday. It was Jessica looking on with a face full of interest. I saw her clearly although I wasn't sure if she could see me. I wanted to call to her, ask her where she's been all this time, but what if she wasn't real? I didn't want to sound like an idiot. Better to keep my mouth shut, at least for now.

Jessica floated through the floor. She was gone as if she was never there at all. I couldn't know how much of this was happening or if my brain was playing tricks on me because of Copeland's spell, or whatever he was doing to me. I had to guess it was mostly tricks. I wasn't really outside, even if it seemed so real.

"Okay, Sam," Copeland's voice went through my head. "Can you still feel the air blowing through your body and the grass against your sneakers?"

"I...I can." Wow, that was no lie, I really could.

"I want you to look down at the grass. There, you will see a door on the grass. Together, we are going to open that door." There was a knock from the door while Copeland spoke. "Behind that door, we will find the answer to all your questions. I want you to reach for the knob and pull the door open."

I reached out for the doorknob. There was suddenly a second knock, this one stronger than the first. But the sound wasn't coming from the door, it was behind me. The grass disappeared along with the door and the sky. The only thing I felt was groggy, as if I had just awakened from a long dream. I peeked over my shoulder to see Copeland walking to his office door.

"I'm sorry, Sam. I tried to wave them off." Copeland opened the door to Kaela and a lady with short brown hair, two chins, and a scowl on her face. Kaela stormed past Copeland, rolling her eyes, and pulling at her own braided hair.

"Good afternoon, Ms. Keening," Copeland said,

through what had to be a fake smile. "What can I do for the two of you?"

Kaela eyed me in the chair, then looked back at Copeland with confusion. "What were you doing in here?"

"Um, nothing huge. Just practicing some counseling techniques."

"You really do that after we leave?"

"Mister Copeland!" Keening's voice nearly shook the entire office. "I need this young lady's disrespect in my class addressed!"

"What disrespect?" Kaela scoffed. "I did your dumb assignment. Jeeze."

"Okay, ladies, relax." Copeland waved his hands in a plunging motion to tell them both to calm down. "Let's start with you, Ms. Keening. What's going on?"

Keening opened her mouth, ready to answer. Kaela cut her off. "She complaining I didn't do her stupid assignment, but I did."

"The assignment was an opinion essay on our recent readings on Romeo and Juliet." Ms. Keening faced Copeland. "Kaela's paper had two words on it only. She wrote, 'It's stupid.' That does not constitute an opinion."

"It is, too, an opinion," Kaela scoffed.

To be honest, it sounded like an opinion to me.

"Kaela, tell me the truth." Copeland turned to face the girl who was pacing from one end of the office to the other. "Were you able to follow the story? I know I had issues with Shakespeare's writing back when I was in high school—"

"I followed the story just fine!" Kaela sucked her teeth. "Some spoiled rich chick kills herself because she don't get what she wants. And we're supposed to give a damn about her?"

"Do you see what I'm talking about, Mr. Copeland?" Keening screeched.

I know I sure didn't. Her description made me laugh. Luckily, only Copeland heard me. He glanced my way. I ran my fingers across my lips as if I was zipping them up.

"There are a lot better reasons for a girl to want to kill herself." Kaela waved a dismissive hand at Keening. "Not like Romeo's the only boy in the entire world, right? But she wanted to be with him, her daddy said no, so she drank poison." Kaela's head sprang toward Copeland. "That's why she's stupid and the whole book is *stupid!*"

"I have to be honest with you, Ms. Keening." Copeland cupped his hands together like he was expecting to get attacked for what he was about to say. "Her interpretation, while unpopular, and maybe a tad crude, does show an intelligent understanding of the story."

"Exactly!" I threw a finger out toward Kaela, then gave her a thumbs-up.

"I am all for teaching critical thinking, Mr. Copeland." Keening shook her head in disgust. "But her belief that Romeo and Juliet is 'stupid' is certainly not a reason for her not to do the assignment."

"I do agree with that." Copeland threw his arm over Kaela's shoulders and walked her closer to Keening. "Since she does have a valid opinion on the story, how about if she writes that opinion in an essay tonight for homework and hands it in first thing tomorrow? Would you accept it and give her credit for the assignment?"

Keening exhaled. "I suppose."

"Great." Copeland led Kaela to the door. "Since it is late, Kaela, why don't you head home and start working on that essay?"

"Whatever." Kaela stormed past Keening and out of the office.

Keening faced Copeland with that nasty scowl so many students who were stuck in her classroom received for just about any reason. "Mr. Copeland, if I may say—"

"We can readdress this tomorrow," Copeland said to Keening with some force in his tone. Taking the hint, she exited the office. Copeland about-faced. "Okay, let's get back to you. Tell me what you experienced."

"Wow..." If I could blink my eyes, I would have. It was all fading from my brain. All I could remember were bits and pieces. "I'm not sure. I want to but..."

"Try."

I tensed, trying to hold onto what I could remember. I floated off the chair. "I think my feet touched grass, if that makes sense. And I saw...someone I used to know. I think it was Jess."

"More importantly, Sam." Copeland walked up to me. "You touched the back of my hand."

"I did what?" I tilted my head.

Copeland reached for my left hand. His fingers flew straight through. "This hand swiped against mine. I felt it, meaning you were able to physically touch me, if only for a moment. After that, your body was once again intangible."

I held my left hand in front of my face. "We just did this. Why can't I remember everything that happened?"

"That can occur with hypnosis, Sam." Copeland leaned his back against the desk with his arms folded. "That's why we used the technique for interrogation. We'd put irate prisoners into a state of calmness. Then we gain information they wouldn't remember sharing with us."

"What did I tell you?"

"Nothing." Copeland groaned. "We were just getting to that part of the process when we were interrupted."

I looked up at Copeland with a huge grin. "Can we try it again?"

"It's getting late." He chuckled. "Let's try it another time, okay?"

"Sure, another time." I took the hint and went for the ceiling, which was my usual exit from Copeland's office. A thought hit me. It caused a feeling, like a wave of—I wasn't sure—amazement? Maybe love, or something like it. I stopped mid-phase and looked down at Copeland.

His head flung toward me once he realized I hadn't left. "Something more on your mind, Sam?"

"I was thinking…I never had a dad." I opened my eyes wide and grinned. I knew telling him this was risky, but I felt like I had to. "You may be the closest thing to me."

Wow, I can't believe I said it. It made Copeland smile. Then, he laughed. Talk about a mixed message. "You realize, Sam, if you were still alive, you'd be forty-three years old right now? I'm only two years older than you."

"Hmm, I never thought about it like that. I'm an

old man!"

We laughed for what felt like forever.

"I wouldn't call you old. What would that make me?" Copeland snorted. "Have a good night, Sam. Try to spend the night working on some of those exercises we've discussed."

"I will, Mr. Copeland. See you tomorrow." I left the office knowing I'd be here bright and early in the morning. Maybe we could try that hypnosis thing again.

Chapter Thirteen

Morning came a bit faster than usual. It was fifteen minutes after eight a.m. when the double doors leading to the main lobby flew open. Dozens of students, and even some staff, scampered through the first-floor hallway. They talked, they laughed, and they entered their classrooms. That meant the breakfast period was over and the day was about to begin. A few students walked straight through me, never realizing I was in front of them. Amazing how that freaked me out the first time it happened. At this point, I was used to it.

I floated into Copeland's office, hoping to have a chance to talk some more before he started his daily sessions. Maybe we could schedule time later today to perform the hypnosis thing again. I'd love to do it this morning, but Copeland was probably going to say to wait until the end of the day. If we tried any earlier, our session would be interrupted before it even started, which seemed to happen a lot to Mr. Copeland.

He was typing away on his computer. "Hey, Mr. Copeland," I announced, forgoing the usual attempt to catch him by surprise. That never worked anyway.

"Good morning, Sam." His eyes stayed on the monitor. His finger speed on that keyboard was amazing to see. "How was your evening?"

"I spent it doing everything you said." I pulled up my legs so I could balance mid-air on my knees. "First,

I remembered a happy time in my life. It was the day my mom took me to the beach when I was ten. I made some friends there who were visiting from a nearby town. We spent the whole day playing frisbee on the sand."

"That does sound like fun." Copeland folded his hands, his typing apparently done. "What about the other activity we discussed?"

"Yeah, I stood in front of the mirror in the teacher's bathroom. I kept saying the reason I couldn't see myself is because I'm dead. I accepted that fact, just like you said I should." I waved my hands from the top of my head to my legs. "I guess that didn't work because I'm still here."

"Are you really accepting it, Sam?" Copeland rested his clenched hands under his chin. "Or are you still in denial about being dead?"

"Denial?" I raised my eyebrows. I was sure he didn't mean it to sound like he was calling me stupid, but it sure sounded that way to me. "Do you think that after twenty-eight years as a ghost, I don't think I'm dead?"

"It doesn't matter what I think, Sam. It matters what you think."

"I think…I know…I'm not alive anymore." I pushed my hand through the desk. "I can't touch anything, I can't eat anything, most people can't see or hear me—"

A deafening explosion from outside the office shook me. I spun my head to the door. Although the bang was a distance away, it definitely came from within the building. So did the multiple screams which followed.

"What the hell was that?" I gasped.

A second bang brought Copeland to his feet. His body became stiff and attentive. "That was an AK-74."

"A what?"

"An assault rifle!"

Copeland ran around his desk, pulled open the door, then dashed through. Wow, if Copeland was right about the sound—and he seemed sure—instead of hiding under his desk like any normal person, the guy charged out of the office and ran toward the gunshot. No wonder I was amazed by him. He was braver and more assured than anyone I'd ever known. I followed Copeland into the hallway where both students and adults were gawking toward the two double doors at the end of the hallway.

"Everyone in your classrooms, *immediately*!" Copeland shouted at the top of his lungs. "This is a hard lockdown. Lock your doors, turn off the lights, and stay hidden!"

"I'll go check it out!" After Copeland nodded at me, I swam to the end of the hallway and through the double doors.

Once in the main lobby, I stopped short and gasped. Two safety officers were on the ground surrounded by puddles of blood. The shooter, a husky man with a white tank-top to show off his hairy and muscular arms, stood in front of the front glass doors over the body of one of the safety officers. A huge rifle, with smoke pouring from the muzzle, sat in his two hands.

The officer was laid out on the floor, shaking and clutching his chest. At least that meant he was still alive. Well, so far. With his back to me, the shooter put the sole of his massive boot across the officer's throat. His head dipped so he could look straight down at the man's panic-filled eyes.

"You were probably a kid when I went to this school, if you were even alive." The shooter's words slurred. His voice was eerily familiar. "You probably went here, too. Look what it did to me. What it turned me into."

"No, it couldn't be," I whispered to myself. "Please, don't be who I think you are…"

"The last time I walked into this place, I never went home." His foot pressed down. The officer gagged. "Now, no one else goes home, either."

He slowly turned away from the body and marched toward the doors behind me. His face was covered by long black facial hair. Clutching the rifle in one hand, he wiped the hair from his face. I gasped. He was much older and bigger than I remembered, but I knew those widened angry eyes and that frown. Man, I didn't want to be right, but I knew I was the moment I heard that voice. I heard it screaming while those demented eyes stared into mine. It was the day life was literally choked out of my body.

"Holy crap!" I squawked.

It was Kurt Baker. He had the same insane and angry look on his face as the day he murdered me. This time, he'd killed two others, and that was just the beginning. I twirled around and flew through the doors as fast as I could. I stopped in front of Copeland who was checking the classroom doors, making sure the handles wouldn't turn.

"Mr. Copeland!" I screamed. "It's him, it's him!"

"What? Him who?"

"It's Kurt!" I waved my hand at the door. "He's huge now, he's going to kill everyone here, and he's coming this way!"

Copeland's eyes narrowed. He ran to the doors as if a switch inside of him had flipped. Copeland stepped to the left of the doors and crouched with his backside against the wall.

"Please be careful, Mr. Copeland!"

My body moved backward as if I was caught in a stiff wind. To my surprise, there was no worry on Copeland's face. He looked as if he had done something like this before. Many times, even.

The doors flung open. Copeland jumped into action, grabbing the rifle from the left side with both hands. He yanked it, and Kurt, forward. An elbow to the nose staggered the angry shooter.

"Yes!" I threw my arms in the air. "Take him down, Mr. Copeland!"

Kurt was even bigger than I realized—he matched Copeland's height. His arms had also inflated; the guy must have lifted a ton of weights in prison. Kurt's widened eyes showed he didn't expect to get ambushed. Copeland snatched the rifle from Kurt's grip and sent it flying across the floor. A right hook to the jaw threw Kurt against the wall. Copeland stepped back and jumped into a defensive stance with his fists clenched and his legs spread.

"It's over, Baker." Copeland's tone was calm but strong. "Stand down."

Kurt lunged. Copeland raised his foot and caught him just below the chest with the sole of his shoe. His attacker toppled back, slamming off the wall. Another threatening strike was halted when the counselor raised his clenched fist.

"We don't have to do this, Kurt," Copeland said. "We can stop right now."

"N-no, you don't understand." Kurt's head shook at a rapid pace. He glared at Copeland with deep and deranged eyes. "It's this school's fault." His voice was barely a whisper. "Sixteen years in prison, no job, no family. All because of this goddamned place."

"You're on something, I can tell." Copeland opened his fist. He showed his palm, a signal for Kurt to stay back. "Relax. We'll get through this together, we'll figure out how to end this in a peaceful—"

"We won't. We can't." Kurt's slurred moan rose to a screech. "Everyone must die!"

His head dropped. The guy was actually sobbing. He suddenly didn't look like the monster who tortured me, killed me, and was now here to kill everyone in the school. He looked like a sad child. A very big one, but a child nonetheless. Copeland must have realized it too; his body loosened up. He moved in and placed a hand on Kurt's shoulder.

"You need help, Kurt," he said in a calm tone. "We can get that help for you—"

Kurt sprang forward like a cat, shoving Copeland. The soldier-turned-counselor staggered. Then his foot slipped out from under him. Copeland dropped to his backside.

"Oh no!" I shouted. "Mr. Copeland, you have to get up!"

Copeland pushed his upper body off the floor. "Damn slippery dress shoes," he mumbled.

Kurt reached behind his waistband and pulled out a pistol, which he aimed at Copeland's face. "You all have to die," Kurt shouted. "Everyone. No exceptions. Starting with you."

Copeland gawked at the barrel of the gun several inches from his face. Kurt's trigger finger shook. Copeland's eyes narrowed with both determination and worry. His hands slowly moved forward while he pulled one leg under his body. I could tell he was trying to figure out a path of attack, but he'd never be able to grab Kurt's gun-holding hand before taking a bullet between the eyes. I had to do something. But I was a ghost. What could I possibly do?

Instinct took over. I hovered to Kurt's right and screamed, "Get away from him!"

Kurt's head spun my way. His eyes were wide, and not just from whatever drugs were running through his body. "What the hell?" His head shot up and down. "*You!*"

"That's right, it's me!" I floated high above his head. "You killed me, Kurt. Today, I'm the ghost of Pinedale High…and I'm here to haunt you."

Kurt snarled like a wild animal seeking its prey. He aimed the gun at me and fired. The bullet passed straight through me and dug into the wall. People screamed from behind classroom doors.

"My whole life," he growled. "Everything! It was all your fault!"

"*My* fault?" My ghostly jaw nearly popped off my mouth and hit the floor. "You choked me until I died. You got exactly what you deserved!"

"No! You did this. You're the reason—"

In one motion, Copeland hopped to his feet and charged, moving in close. He snatched Kurt's wrist with one hand and slammed a karate chop to his elbow with the other. Kurt's arm bent so the gun-holding hand was aimed under their chins. Kurt's free hand clutched Copeland by the throat. The two struggled like wrestlers trying to take each other down.

"It's over, Kurt," Copeland roared. "Let the gun go! It's your only chance—"

"*Never!*" Kurt cackled like a raving lunatic. "*It all has to end here, now!*"

Both men screamed with rage. The gun went off.

I turned my head away from the booming explosion that filled the hallway. More screams came from behind the classroom doors, several at the least. I didn't see who won that struggle. All I knew was that the grunting from both men had stopped. Oh God, if Copeland was the one who was shot, I'd spend the rest of eternity with guilt stabbing me in the chest like a dagger I could never tug loose…

After several long moments, I willed myself to look. Copeland was on his knees, covered in blood. The sight of his shirt drowned in red stains made me gasp.

But it wasn't his blood. Kurt was on the floor, facedown, his head and upper body surrounded by a river of crimson red. The gun was still clutched in his hand, with smoke pouring from the barrel.

"Mr. Copeland," I shrieked. "Are you all right? Please tell me you're all right!"

"I'm fine." He stood and gazed behind him at the empty hallway, then down at the body. "This looks like a suicide. Better that way."

Before I could ask "why," Copeland scurried backward, then kicked the rifle. It slid across the floor, stopping at Kurt's side.

Copeland wiped a hand across his face, scraping

off a layer of Kurt's blood from his chin and cheeks. His head popped toward the double doors leading to the main lobby. "Do you hear that?"

"Hear what?"

"Boots stomping on the floor. It's the police entering the building. It could be a S.W.A.T. team." He stared at his blood-covered fingers. "Let me get out of Dodge and clean this off." He ran into the student bathroom. The door closed behind him.

I passed through the doors and entered the lobby. Copeland was right. Eight huge police officers in helmets, face shields, and thick vests entered through the front door, their rifles aimed in all directions. Two dropped to check on the injured safety officers. As the rest spread out to the various attached hallways, I pointed in the direction they needed to go. "He's this way!" I shouted. "Over here!"

Of course, none of them could see or hear me. But with the threat over, I knew they'd find their way eventually.

Chapter Fourteen

To my surprise, school was open the next day. I really thought the place would be shut down for a while after a shooting, but education must go on, I guess. Things were busier than usual, or at least it felt that way. The few students who came in walked into the building slowly and with a hesitation in their step. I totally got why; Hank the custodian hadn't even cleaned all the bloodstains off the floor, at least not yet. Even I was more anxious than normal at this time of the morning, but there was a reason for my nerves. After everything that happened, it wasn't over yet, at least not for one person.

Finally, the guy I was waiting for stepped through the doors and into the school's vestibule. He had his usual breakfast in a brown paper bag in his left hand, a newspaper under his arm, and a cup of steaming coffee in his right hand. Too bad he wouldn't have the chance to enjoy any of it, and he needed to know that right away.

"Mr. Copeland!" I floated to the front doors and stopped in front of him where I said his name again.

"What is it, Sam?" Copeland's shoulders fell back. "What's the matter? You look like you've seen a…well…"

Copeland waved his coffee at me. I wasn't sure if he was making another joke or not, but it didn't matter.

There was a way bigger issue he was about to face.

"There's two guys in the principal's office. They're asking about you." I waved both hands toward the hallway which led to the principal's office. "They look, like, really important."

"Important? What do you mean by 'important'?"

"They're wearing dark suits and ties. They flashed badges in leather wallets—"

"Mr. Copeland!" Principal Kouriki's voice boomed through the main lobby. She said it with such concern that others stopped and looked her way. She stood next to the door outside the hallway leading to her office. Her eyes were wider than they'd ever been before. It made sense with everything her school had been through yesterday. Despite it all, she still kept that professional "I'm in charge" scowl across her face.

Copeland faced her with his shoulders yanked back. He nodded, then marched like a soldier about to face a firing squad. I followed as Kouriki led Copeland into her office's hallway. Soon, we were in front of her office, which was the biggest one in the school. I wasn't sure what I could do to help, but I didn't want to leave Copeland alone.

Kouriki unlocked then opened the door. I floated past Copeland and entered first. A stocky man with gray hair and dark sunglasses sat in the principal's chair behind the huge desk. Until today, I've never seen anyone else but Kouriki, or whoever was the principal at the time, sitting in that cushioned leather chair. No matter who held that title, they always treated the chair like a throne in their castle. Yet, this man sat as if he owned the thing.

"You're Jack Copeland." He said the name more as

a statement than a question.

"Yes, that's me." Copeland placed his newspaper, paper bag, and coffee, on top of the end table by the suede couch facing the desk.

"Good morning. Please have a seat," the man said, with an authority that put Kouriki's to shame.

The second man, a tall guy in a dark suit, with bleached blond hair and a tablet in his hands, stood to the left of the desk. A pair of dark sunglasses peeked out from the jacket pocket near his chest. They looked exactly like the one on the face of the guy in the chair. Kouriki moved to the end of the couch and sat. She waved Copeland to join her, which, after a moment's hesitation, he did.

He straightened his back against the couch. "Um, how can I help you?" Copeland wore a slight smirk on his face.

"I don't think they're looking for help," I whispered. Copeland flicked his right hand, a signal for me to keep my lips zipped.

The man in the chair dropped his badge on the table. "I'm Lieutenant Avery Banks with the Federal Bureau of Investigation. This is Detective Michael Stahl. He is running the follow-up on the incident which took place yesterday in this school."

"Good to know." Copeland leaned forward. "May I ask about the two safety officers who were injured? How are they?"

"The officer who took the initial bullet to the chest is in critical condition," Stahl explained. "The other officer was shot in the right bicep. No vital organs were hit. He is expected to make a full recovery."

"Let's hope for the best for both of them."

Copeland folded his hands in his lap. "Now, why am I here?"

"We have a few details we need to go over before closing this case." Something in the lieutenant's voice was suspicious. The fact that even I picked up on it meant he wasn't trying too hard to hide it.

"I presumed that case was closed. Kurt Baker killed himself."

Detective Stahl cleared his throat. "That is how it looked at the time, Mr. Copeland. However, we have some details to confirm before we close the case. Let's start with your whereabouts when the incident took place."

"Meaning?"

The detective's eyes narrowed to the point the ridges in his forehead looked like squiggly lines on a pyramid. He spoke deliberately slow and with attitude. "Where were you at the time Kurt Baker roamed through the building?"

Copeland's eyes flashed toward me in the corner, then back to Stahl. "I was in the student restroom with the door locked. I was walking through the hallway when I heard the first gun shot. I immediately called for a hard lockdown, then went for cover where I could."

Stahl exchanged a glance with the lieutenant, then with Kouriki. The principal's foot tapped a nervous beat against the tiled floor. A gust of air flew out of Stahl's nostrils as he planted his intense gaze on Copeland. "Did you, at any point, confront the shooter?"

The principal shifted to face Copeland, who pressed his back against the cushion. Copeland licked his lips. I expected him to tell them what happened, but it was clear he didn't want to. I couldn't understand why; the man was a hero, yet he didn't want them to know. There had to be a reason.

"I'm not sure where you're going with this," Copeland answered after a long pause. "A man entered this school, shot two safety officers, then himself. Why would you think I confronted him? It's not like a counseling session was going to stop him, right?" Copeland laughed, which made things even more awkward.

Banks waved his hand to the desk. In response, Stahl balanced his tablet across the desk with the screen facing Copeland and Kouriki. "As part of our investigation, we went through the school's security footage from the last twenty-four hours." He tapped the screen. "What we saw disputes your claim that you stayed hidden. In fact, the camera captured quite an impressive performance."

I floated in front of Kouriki, knowing I wouldn't block her view. I wanted to see what the cameras caught on tape. It was a video of Copeland wrestling the rifle from Kurt, the elbow he threw to Kurt's nose, and the kick to his gut. It was gray, maybe even a bit blurry, but it was clear who was on the screen. The camera even caught Kurt trying to shoot me, although without me in the footage, it was just him shooting the wall.

We watched the struggle for the pistol in Kurt's hand and Copeland forcing it under his opponent's chin as it went off. Blood sprayed everywhere like a water faucet that suddenly exploded. It was a brutal sight that, even on the screen, made me turn away.

Kouriki's hand flew over her mouth. "Oh, my

goodness."

"Uh-oh," I gasped. "They know! You're so screwed!"

The screen went blank. All eyes, including mine, looked Copeland's way.

I floated into a sitting position at the edge of the desk. Copeland glanced around the room like he was trying to find an answer they'd accept. He threw up his hands in defeat. "Okay, yes. I stopped Kurt Baker before he could shoot anyone else, which was clearly his intent. I gave him every chance to stand down, but he made it clear he had no intention of doing so. He was going to kill everybody."

"That's exactly what happened!" I yelled.

"I don't understand." Principal Kouriki rested a hand on Copeland's shoulder. "You prevented a massacre yesterday. Why hide what you did?"

"Because he has to; he has no choice." Banks' rough tone nearly shook me out of midair. It also grabbed the attention of everyone in the room. "Am I right, Mr. Copeland?"

"I'm not sure what you mean, Lieutenant," Copeland replied, not taking the bait.

"Of course, you do." Banks leaned forward and placed his elbows against the desk. "I'm an ex-military vet myself. Back in my youth, I had the opportunity to train for one of our country's top special ops units.

"Admittedly, I didn't make it in, most of us didn't, but I gained a few friends who did. Even after my rejection, I worked out and sparred with them in the gym. They let me in on some of the training, so they'd have an extra sparring partner." Banks waved a hand above the tablet. "Their techniques were smooth. Much like the ones I saw in that recording. When disarming a pistol, they always grabbed the wrist, then the elbow. They practiced it on a regular basis."

"What are you getting at, Lieutenant?" Copeland crossed his arms and gave Banks a suspicious glance.

The abnormally tall Detective Stahl waltzed around the desk and stopped in front of the couch. He removed a notepad from his chest pocket and held it in front of his face. "I was informed this is your first year as a school counselor, Mr. Copeland. You started just over six weeks ago after a career in the military. Is that correct?"

"Yes, that's accurate." Copeland eyed me, then the principal. Kouriki stared back at him with intense curiosity. He stood up and faced the detective who had a few inches over him. "After my retirement, I finished my schooling and earned my school counseling license. That's all on record. I interviewed with Principal Kouriki, and she hired me right away. That's when I moved to Pinedale to begin my new career."

"Interesting sequence of events." Stahl flipped a page on his notepad. "Even more interesting, your interview with Principal Kouriki took place just three days after Kurt Baker was released from prison. That's one hell of a coincidence."

"What does that mean?" Kouriki's question was followed by an eerie silence.

I floated face-to-face with Copeland, who walked through me and up to Stahl. The two locked eyes. After a momentary faceoff, Stahl stepped back.

"According to your record, Mr. Copeland, since you started here at Pinedale High School, you have a perfect attendance."

"It's hasn't been that long, Lieutenant," Copeland replied. "And I do believe in being here and doing my job—"

"*Or* is it possible you were waiting for something? Perhaps someone." Stahl tapped his notepad with a pencil like one of those police detectives during an interrogation. "Did you have prior knowledge that Kurt Baker was planning to come to this building upon his release from prison?"

"Did you?" I asked. I was sure Copeland wasn't here as a spy all along, but it did make a little bit of sense, at least it did the way Detective Stahl presented the timeline.

"Ah, so that's your working theory." Copeland grinned in the face of Stahl. "I state, as a matter of fact, that I never knew who Kurt Baker was until yesterday. No, I am not here undercover, if that is what you're specifically asking. I am no longer employed, affiliated, or associated with our military, or our government, in any capacity other than as a veteran. I am a civilian, and my occupation is school counselor for the students at Pinedale Central High School."

"I see." Stahl placed the notepad and pencil back into his chest pocket. "So, Kurt Barton simply chose the wrong school to try to shoot up as it just happened to have a professionally trained former military operative in its employ? Is that the story?"

"No, detective, that is *not* the story!" Copeland's voice suddenly turned fierce, like a lion roaring at a threat. I never heard such force from him before. From the look of Kouriki's wide-eyed stare, she hadn't either. It was as if the counselor she hired, and had known, had suddenly been replaced by the kick-ass soldier he once was. "The official story is Kurt Barton entered his former high school with weapons, shot two guards, and then himself. Barton killed himself with his handgun. Forensics will back up that story. That would be the cleanest take for all of us."

"You must be joking," Stahl scoffed.

Copeland gave Stahl a threatening glance. "Why would I be joking?"

"Mr. Copeland." Kouriki rose to her feet. She placed a hand on Copeland's elbow, maybe as an attempt to cut the tension, which right now, was at an all-time high. "You are asking us all to lie on official documents and fabricate facts in a federal investigation. We can't legally do that. It would make us all guilty of conspiracy."

To be honest, I didn't understand why Copeland wanted everyone to lie about what happened, but he must have his reasons. His fists clenched at his sides and his cheeks turned red with worry, like he was afraid to get locked up. That would be crazy since the guy did nothing wrong. But, even if they left him alone, what if he decided to leave, anyway? That would be a bad thing because the school needed him. I needed him. I had to do something, but what? How could I possibly help?

My body suddenly tugged. It was as if I was in an ocean and the tide took hold of me. I drifted—not under my control—toward the desk and above Banks' head. I dropped straight down into the lieutenant's body. Everything looked darker, which I quickly realized was from the sunglasses on his face. Almost on instinct, I grabbed the glasses and removed them. It had been so long since I could touch anything that I almost forgot what an object...any object...felt like in my fingers.

The glasses were heavier than I expected.

I stood from my seat and viewed everybody in the room through eyes that were not my own. My feet touched the floor. Wow, this was so cool. Odd, but cool, and so much more real than when Copeland hypnotized me into thinking I felt the floor.

"We can do it!" I said, although the voice wasn't mine. I opened my mouth wide as my hand pressed against my chest, a chest that moved up and down when I breathed. I even felt the smooth fabric of the suit. It was damp from sweat and had a musty smell to it.

"Lieutenant?" Stahl leaned forward. "Are you okay?"

"I am okay." My lips stretched into a slight grin. Realizing I was hunching, I straightened my back and stood at attention. "And I say we go with the Kurt killed himself story."

"Lieutenant Banks, if I may…" Kouriki raised a finger. "Even if we match our stories, the video footage contradicts it completely—"

"We can erase it," Copeland interrupted. "The suicide story is simple, it's clean, and it leaves far less questions for any of us to answer. Is it accurate to say no one else has seen that video except for the people in this room?"

"So far, it is," Stahl answered. "But still…"

Kouriki and Stahl gazed my way. At first, the focus on me made me gulp as if they caught me and I was in trouble. Then I remembered, they couldn't know it was me. As far as they knew, I was the adult in charge. To them, I was Lieutenant Banks. I flicked a finger at Copeland. "Yes, what he said."

"We're absolutely sure about this?" the detective

asked me with a cloud of suspicion and concern.

I pulled back my shoulders, trying to look official, whatever that meant. "Mr. Copeland saved a lot of lives yesterday, Mister…um, Detective Stahl. It wouldn't be fair to get him in trouble for it. Oh, also, the questions thing."

Kouriki raised a finger. "We would have to lie—"

"It's not a lie if we all accept it as truth," Copeland said, cutting her off. "The official story is Kurt Barton killed himself, bringing his rampage to a halt."

"I agree!" I clapped my hands together. It made a popping sound. I hadn't been able to do that since I was alive. I rubbed my hands against the stubble on my cheeks, but quickly pulled them away before Stahl and the principal looked back at me. "Erase the video," I said.

Stahl let out a deep sigh. "Very well, Lieutenant. Despite my hesitation, I suppose this is the cleanest path for us to take." He turned the tablet his way and tapped his finger twice against the screen. "The video is erased. Kurt Barton's death is officially ruled a suicide. Thank you all for your time."

I leapt into the air, leaving the lieutenant's body. At first, he looked around, scratching the side of his head. With a clear hobble in his step, Banks walked to the door. Stahl reached for the knob, but then looked over his shoulder at Copeland. "One last question, if I may?"

Copeland nodded. "What's your question?"

"Yeah," I screeched. "What question?" Maybe I left the lieutenant's body too soon?

"Satisfy my curiosity." Stahl let the door swing closed behind him. "I noticed on the video, Kurt Baker had you dead to rights. Then, he looked to the left, and panicked. It appeared like he was talking to someone who wasn't there. That gave you the opportunity to overtake him. Any idea what spooked him?"

"Oh, crap!" I shouted.

Copeland shrugged. "He was on something heavy. I saw it in his eyes. I'm guessing Baker was suffering some sort of drug-induced hallucination. Lucky me, right? If not, this could have all gone badly. Then we wouldn't be here having this conversation."

I spread my arms with a huge grin. "I'm what spooked him."

"No, we would not." Stahl straightened his back, brought his right hand to his forehead, and saluted. "Thank you for your time, Mr. Copeland. Best of luck to you."

"Thank you."

Copeland returned the salute. I did the same, even if only Copeland could see it. Stahl pulled the door by the knob and held it open for Banks to walk ahead of him. The lieutenant was still clutching his forehead. My fault, I guess. The door slammed shut behind both men.

"If you don't mind, Principal Kouriki." Copeland made a dash for the door. "I'd like to get back to work."

Kouriki stepped in Copeland's path to the office's door. "I guess your secret is safe, Mr. Copeland. Although I admit, I am confused as to why that is necessary. What you did yesterday was certainly not a criminal act. In fact, if not for you and you alone, it would have been a most tragic day, one from which the town of Pinedale may never have recovered."

"She's right," I said, at the top of my lungs. "You're a hero, Mr. Copeland!"

He looked back and forth at both of us. "Upon my

retirement from service, it was made crystal clear to me the skills I learned were to be used on our military's behalf, and not meant for the civilian world." Copeland maneuvered around Kouriki, moving to the doorway. "Should it get out what actually happened yesterday, I would have to answer to people much higher up the chain than Lieutenant Banks. That's a scenario I'd much rather avoid."

"Even if those skills were used to save potentially hundreds of lives, many of which are children?"

Copeland exhaled, then looked to the ceiling. "Let's just say it's best I don't take that chance. There are those who would see my engagement into the situation only as a violation of my separation agreement from my old position."

"Okay, Mr. Copeland." Kouriki let loose a half-smile. "I understand."

"Do you really?"

"Honestly, no, but you've certainly earned your privacy." The principal placed a hand on Copeland's elbow. "And my gratitude." She let out a deep exhale. "In truth, you've earned the gratitude of the entire town of Pinedale, even if no one but us will ever know it."

"I'll know, too!" I shouted.

Copeland replied, "I can live with that."

Kouriki stepped aside and waved to the door. Copeland snatched his belongings from the end table and left the office. I floated through the wall so I could catch up to him.

Chapter Fifteen

The moment we entered the counseling office, Copeland kicked the door shut and dropped his breakfast into the trashcan next to his desk. I guess he just didn't have the stomach to eat after the confrontation in the principal's office. He leaned against the wall and let out a deep sigh of relief.

"Well, that was a close one." He stared at me as if he was seeing me for the first time. "Possession. I didn't realize you could do that."

"I didn't know either. It was kind of weird, right?" I chuckled louder than I ever had before, at least until I caught his skeptical blue eyes. "That was the first time I did anything like that. I'm not even sure how it happened. Honest."

Copeland nodded. "Well, whatever you did, you saved my ass. Again. So, thank you."

"You're welcome." The ends of my lips touched my ears. It meant a lot that Copeland was so happy with me for what I did. "We made a pretty good team stopping Kurt like that, didn't we?"

"Yes, I guess we did." Copeland laughed. "Who would have thought a retired soldier and the ghost of a fifteen-year-old student would save the day?"

"Man, that would make a great TV show, don't you think?" My arms flailed in the air like a bird as I floated, nearly passing through the ceiling. "The soldier and the ghost. That would be so freakin' cool—"

Suddenly, a jolt whipped through my body as if something shocked me. Then my body tugged. This one was stronger than the pull I felt when I entered Lieutenant Banks. Was I entering Copeland's body? He was the only one in the room with me. No, it wasn't that. Somehow, this was different. I was just a couple of yards away from him.

The pull became stronger, to the point I was no longer in control of my arms and legs. I had a hunch what was going on, even if I didn't expect it to happen…I guess I knew it had to happen eventually, but I never thought it would be so sudden.

"Mr. Copeland." My voice was barely above a whisper.

"Yes, Sam?" Copeland looked up at me. The grin left his face. "What's the matter?"

"I think it's time for me to go."

"What do you mean?"

I needed to fight it just for the moment, at least long enough so I could say goodbye. Mr. Copeland deserved that much.

"To pass." I held my hand in front of my face. It was lighter and more transparent than ever before. "I'm ready to go to…whatever's next. I know there's probably nothing next, but I'm ready all the same."

Copeland stared at me without saying a word. There wasn't much he could say. "Good luck" didn't fit this situation. He nodded, then stepped back, his eyes never leaving mine.

"It was great meeting you, sir." I couldn't hear my own voice. "Thank you for helping me."

"Likewise," Copeland answered with a grin. "I

won't forget yo—"

Copeland's lips moved, but I couldn't hear a sound. Not from him, not from the office's air conditioner, nothing. My vision blurred. I couldn't make out Copeland's body. It was like looking at him through a water bubble. All of a sudden, I couldn't make him out, or the rest of the room, at all. It was time to die, and I was okay with that.

In the end, it was a decent life, and a not a terrible afterlife…

Chapter Sixteen

The next morning...

As a special ops soldier, I experienced things no one else would believe or could ever understand...no one except my squad. Yesterday, however, took new experiences to a whole different level. Taking down a terrorist certainly wasn't new—although I never expected to have to engage one after I retired, or in a school—but considering who assisted me in that crisis, I'd say it qualified as new territory. Time to put it behind me and move on.

The best way to do that was to go through my day and keep things normal, so I followed my usual morning routine. I stopped by The Bodega a mile down the road from my ranch-style home and ordered my usual toasted bagel with scrambled eggs, ham, and cheese. The deli owner, Pedro Santana, had my sandwich ready for me along with my cup of black coffee and newspaper. It was nice to be able to walk into his place, and Pedro always had my order ready because he knew my daily schedule. It was one aspect of small-town life I appreciated.

It was time to take my fast-paced walk to Pinedale Central High School in the center of town. It was a six-mile walk. In fact, everything in Pinedale was within six miles of the high school, which, with two floors, was the town's second tallest building outside of the apartment building a few blocks away from my ranch house. What a difference from the city where I grew up, for better or worse. To think, when I first moved here, I thought I was leaving all sorts of craziness behind in exchange for the quiet life.

I entered the school building the same time as usual, six a.m. I was ready to start a new day in my role as counselor, a day I hoped would feel far more than normal than it had been since I began my new career. Sam, my most interesting student, because he was a ghost, had moved on. It wasn't likely I'd ever see him again, but hopefully he was resting comfortably, wherever he may be.

I rubbed my eyes and yawned. I had been up most of the night thinking about him, and I did so with a feeling of satisfaction. It took twenty-eight years, but he finally stood up to his bully. In doing so, he saved a lot of lives and was able to move to whatever experiences were next. Principal Kouriki gave me her gratitude and I accepted the compliment. In truth, I disagreed. Sam was the true hero. If it wasn't for him, I'd most likely be dead, and so would many others. Then maybe we'd all have become ghosts haunting this school, trying to find a path to the other side—

"You look deep in thought, Mr. Hero."

The gruff voice spun me around with a clenched fist. I guess I was still a bit jumpy, plus not too many of my colleagues came in as early as I did each day.

"Oh, yes, my apologies. I was lost in thought." I played it off with a laugh. "Good morning, Hank."

"Good morning, Mr. Copeland." Hank dropped the business-end of the mop he held into the wheeled bucket filled with dirty water and soap suds. Hank was the only one who beat me into the building each and every day. He came in so early there were times I suspected he slept in his car in the parking lot.

"So, how are you coping this morning after that whole mess?" he asked.

"I'm okay—" I paused. Hank's greeting suddenly hit me. I faked a confused look. "What did you mean by 'hero'? I heard Kurt Barton killed himself."

"Yeah, that's what it said in this morning's newspaper. Most of us were in hiding because of the lockdown and have no idea what really happened." Hank poked me in the chest. "But not all of us. Ain't that right, Mr. Copeland?"

Hank was a short, plump guy with as many rips across his shirt as dirt on his overalls. I couldn't tell his age, but he had to be long past time for retirement. I suspect he had been part of this school even before the furniture. People, especially the students, tended to ignore Hank as he passed through the hallways. I'd almost think he was a ghost, if not for the ammonia-like smell that followed him everywhere. He was a quiet guy, but I had a hunch Hank knew more than he let on. I don't know why I never conversed with him past "good morning" and "have a nice evening." It was time to change that pattern. Plus, it was nice to finally open up to somebody, especially one not wearing a badge, or sitting behind a desk.

I looked directly into Hank's bright blue eyes. "Believe it or not, I met a ghost. He was a student named Sam Anderson from way back. He helped me get the jump on Barton." A snicker forced its way out of my throat. Well, he asked. "Go ahead, tell me I must be crazy. I don't expect anyone to believe that story, anyway."

Now it was Hank's turn to laugh. "It is a tough story to believe. All them ghosts here in Pinedale High School rarely interact with the living, much less get involved. That does include Sam."

"Hold on." My head snapped back. "You knew about him?"

"Watching over this building and keeping it clean, it's all in my job description." Hank shoved the perma-stained mop strands farther down into the bucket. He rolled it past me. "But I think it may be best we keep this story between us, and just go about our day. Wouldn't you agree?"

"We are definitely on the same page, Hank." I tipped my coffee cup his way. "Thanks. And have a nice day."

"You too, Mr. Copeland," Hank shouted from the end of the lobby. "Stay out of trouble, right?"

"Um, right."

I strolled in the opposite direction toward the hallway that led to my office. Hank was a genuinely nice guy. Our conversation was short, but pleasurable. He was easy to talk to. I certainly did not regret sharing the truth with him, although I was surprised how he didn't flinch when I talked about Sam. Then he surprised me, even though what he said meant my gut was right on him. He knew more about this place than he let on. I made a mental note to chat with the guy more often—

"Hold on!"

I spun like a top. "Hank, wait! Did you say ghosts? As in plural?" A door leading to another hallway swung shut. Hank was gone, off to go about his day.

All them ghosts. I was sure I heard him right. He could have been screwing with me, but I had no reason to think that was the case. If what he said was true, then Sam, and the girl ghost Sam mentioned—the one that disappeared long ago—may not have been the only spirits that haunted this school. The idea of that, if it was the case, left me with cause for concern. Deep concern.

What were the others like? Were they also good people, even former students who were lost? Or were they evil and menacing with dark agendas? Maybe they were both, or something in between. Did the rest of the staff know? So far, I hadn't conversed with too many of them. For all I knew, it was the talk of the teacher's lounge, which I rarely frequented.

I haven't heard any stories of other schools being haunted, so why this one? And why was I able to see Sam but no one else could? For that matter, I never saw any other ghosts, at least not yet. What brings out these ghosts? It could be anything, lots of things…or something specific. This was something I'd want to investigate and find out everything I could, if I had the time. The living students, however, kept me busy, so perhaps I wouldn't have that time.

Even as I walked to my office, I couldn't help but look around at the walls and the ceiling, expecting to find another transparent face watching me and looking to chat. Maybe things wouldn't be so ordinary around here after all.

****

The day went by fast. Three o'clock came before I knew it. I hadn't seen any students, and I hadn't touched as much of my paperwork as I had hoped. It wasn't from a lack of trying, but my mind kept wandering back to moments in my life, specifically during a few of my missions as a special ops soldier.

I kept thinking about an early one, when I was in my mid-twenties. I was sent, along with my team, to the west bank in the Middle East. We had information that three important American diplomats were abducted and being held captive in a terrorist-run prison camp. Our mission was to locate them, fight our way out, and get them home safely. Luckily, our intelligence agents were able to pinpoint the exact location of the prison, and we were sent into the territory.

As my team's colonel led us through the prison, we noticed a lack of guards both inside and outside the walls. Because of my youth, and from my lack of experience, I took it as a sign that this would be an easier mission than expected. That was the same thinking of the entire team since our colonel was cocky and my fellow soldiers all shared in my lack of years. It almost cost us our lives. In fact, it should have.

A voice screamed from what I thought was a distance away. The voice was soft, but it clearly said, "Get out." From what I could see from my team and our colonel, I was the only one who heard the warning. The voice spoke again. "Get out while you can!" Once again, no one heard it except for me.

I called for an immediate retreat, yelling for everyone to turn back. "It's a set-up!" I shouted. "Pull out while we can!"

Reacting to my warning, we abandoned the mission and exited the building. Our colonel, confused as he was, followed us out of the prison camp and far from the area. Just as he jumped in my face and questioned my call, which I had no authority to make, the building blew up. The blast caused a percussive wind that knocked us off our feet. A number of injuries resulted from the force of the explosion. I'd landed a few feet away, hitting the ground hard and breaking my right arm. Others in my squad caught fire, but those who remained unscathed were able to put out the flames. Had we been caught in the heart of that explosion instead of just nearby, we would have all been killed instantly.

It turned out the abducted diplomats weren't in there at all. The prison was abandoned. The information we received was fake. It was a set-up meant to cause a huge upset to our government by taking out an entire special forces team with one blow. I was praised and given both a medal and a promotion for my instincts which saved us all. But all I did was heed the warning.

The wreckage was sifted through days later. The search confirmed no one was inside when the bombs went off. Back at base, I consulted a psychiatrist who insisted I must have seen something that warned me. That it was an inner voice giving life to my instincts. In the end, he determined the warning happened in my head caused by momentary paranoia, and it turned out my suspicions were correct. I accepted that answer and moved on. But looking back, I was no longer sure.

Ghosts do exist; I met one right here in Pinedale High. I came to know him well. Could there have been a ghost in that prison camp who issued the warning? Is it possible I didn't earn the medal they pinned to my chest? That question will probably haunt me the rest of my life. I guess I'll never be sure.

The school day had ended two hours ago, and I was still staring at a blank monitor. Perhaps it was time to go home. I stood from my chair and turned off my computer. Once the screen went black, I maneuvered around the desk, heading for the door. Maybe that six-mile stroll home was exactly what I needed to clear my head. On the way, I'd grab a sandwich from The Bodega then watch some TV while I chowed down—

My hand touched the doorknob, but something made me pause. It was an instinct which told me I was being watched. An impossible thought since I was alone in my rather small office, but my training kicked into gear. It created a sixth sense that told me when there were a pair of eyes aimed my way. That gut feeling saved my life, and the lives of my team, many times. Could it be a ghost? I only knew of one.

"Sam?" I spun away from the door at a leopard's pace. It would be unfortunate if, after everything that happened, he didn't move on at all.

Sure enough, I was right about another presence in my office. But it wasn't Sam, not unless he grew his hair long and down his back, changed his skin tone, and put on a gown. A girl the same or close to his age floated between the window and desk. It was another ghost staring at me, and one I found familiar. Strange because I was sure we'd never met before.

"Who are you?" I asked, then waited for an answer. If I could see her, I was sure I could hear her as well.

She floated toward me, passing through my desk. "I'm sorry to have scared you, Mr. Copeland. I did not wish to do that."

"How do you know me?"

"I've been watching you." She waved a hand to the

chairs in front of my desk. "You spent a lot of time talking to yourself. I soon realized you were talking to another ghost like me. I listened in, and you said his name. You were talking to my friend, Sam."

Now I knew why she seemed so familiar. She matched Sam's description perfectly. "You're Jessica, aren't you?"

"Yes. I see Sam told you about me. We were friends, after all. I didn't know him long, yet I miss him terribly. In fact, I think I caused his death."

Sam had told me Jessica was the one who finally convinced him to stand up to Kurt. She wasn't the only one who gave him the advice, but Jessica couldn't have known that. That's why she had guilt written all over her face. It was a specific look I had seen in the mirror many years ago. I felt sympathy for Jessica having to live with such a belief all these years, but this wasn't the time to appease a ghost's feelings. More pressing questions had to come first.

"Sam told me you had been around for a long time. If you were here during my time with him, why couldn't I see you then, but I can see you now?"

"I don't know, Mr. Copeland." She smirked. "I'm a ghost, not a—"

"Not a ghost expert. Right." So she's where Sam got the line.

Jessica gave me a nod. "All I can tell you is I wanted to get to know Sam, so I focused on him. Suddenly, he could see me. Today, I spent every moment focusing on you. Now, we are speaking."

"Is that how it works?"

She shrugged. "I can't say for sure, but it did for you, and for him. On the other hand, I've tried it in the past with others and had no success at all."

That didn't really answer anything for me. I placed my fists against my hips. From her open lips and eye movements, I could tell she was spooked. Ironic since she was a ghost. "What's going on, Jessica? Why do you need to speak with me?"

"Because, in all the time I have roamed these hallways—" her eyes went wide "—I've never come across another ghost. That is until today. He even spoke to me. He said he is here for you, Mr. Copeland."

"I didn't need my gut or my instincts to realize she wasn't talking about Sam. "Who is here, Jessica?" The answer was obvious, but I had to hear it from her.

"It's Kurt. Kurt Baker, the man you killed. He wants you to know his spirit is here in Pinedale High School...and it is seeking you out."

Yup, just the person I expected her to say. Just great. So much for things being ordinary.

Chapter Seventeen

"I could see it in his eyes," Jessica said to me. "I am sure he is here for no good reason."

I stared at the ghost in my office with both disbelief and a hint of frustration. After watching Sam disappear for what I presumed was his spirit being laid to rest, it was time for me to put the whole ghost in the school thing behind me. I should have known huge happenings like this do not simply come to an end. There's always another corner to turn.

"What does Kurt want with me?" I asked, although I did have some idea. Sam was a ghost for twenty-eight years, only moving on when he confronted his killer. Now, Kurt was dead, and I was the one who killed him. My best guess revolved around him looking for a confrontation of his own. With me.

"He didn't say," Jessica replied. "But he is determined to seek you out."

"I'm sure he is." I threw up my hands. "I'm sure I'll have to deal with it at some point in the near future. Perhaps it's time I headed home—"

I spoke too soon. A voice called from the distance. I heard the sound through the door and in the air. It said, "Copeland." It echoed much like the voice in that prison camp before it blew up. Dammit.

I ran past the ghost in my office, pulled open the door, and dashed into the hallway. I looked both ways.

Of course, it was empty.

The voice spoke again. "Copeland." This time, it came from the door at the end of the hallway which led to the main lobby.

Jessica popped from behind the wall. She glided to my side. "Did you hear that?" I asked her.

"I did hear it." There was a shudder in her voice. "That is him, Kurt Baker."

"Of course it is." What else could it be but my actions returning to haunt me?

The voice echoed yet again, calling my name. This time, it was sharper, but it came from the same direction. He was waiting for me in the lobby, and he wanted me to know that. I knew what I had to do. I straightened my back and marched toward the doors. Might as well get this over with—

"Mr. Copeland, wait!" Jessica flew in front of me, waving her hands as if to make me stop. "You do not have to face him."

"I believe I do—"

"No, you don't."

Jessica flexed her head forward with a glance that said her idea was an obvious one. "What are you thinking, Jessica?" I asked.

"Ghosts cannot leave this building, Mr. Copeland. He can only confront you if you choose to stay."

"I thought you weren't a ghost expert."

Jessica shook her head. Check it out, I managed to annoy a ghost. I made a mental note to add that to my resumé of talents.

"I have never been able to leave this building!" She pointed to her chest. "I have never heard any talk of a ghost sighting in Pinedale outside of this school. You can leave, Mr. Copeland. You can just go home. If you do, Kurt cannot follow you, at least I don't believe he can."

"You're telling me to duck out?"

She nodded, then waved her arms toward the door on the opposite end of the hallway. The staircase behind that door led to the emergency exit. "You are not obligated to face him."

Jessica was right. Kurt was stuck here in the school. That meant I only needed to deal with this confrontation if I stayed. Leaving the building and heading straight home did mean Kurt couldn't follow me. Then I wouldn't have to face this ghost and answer to him about his death. At least that's what I presumed this was all about. That strategy, however, also meant I couldn't ever return to this building, never return to work at this school. I'd have to pick up and relocate, perhaps to another area of North Carolina where my state counseling license was valid.

I could hear my old colonel telling me to prove myself and face a threat straight-on. The old me would have jumped at this opportunity. To show that I could stand up to a ghost would bolster my pride in ways I needed back in my youth. But today, it wasn't necessary. I'd proven myself enough on the battlefield and no longer needed to engage an aggressor just for the sake of knowing I could. My self-confidence would remain intact even if I simply walked away.

Then what would happen in this school? If Kurt hadn't come to the school when he did, Sam would still be floating around here, unable to pass over. Maybe that's all Kurt needed to enter total and permanent death as well. If I didn't face him, he could end up haunting this school forever. God help those who had the ability to see and hear him.

No, I couldn't run from this problem and force others—many of whom weren't even born yet—to deal with Kurt Baker's ghost. How could I live with myself if I left it all behind? The responsibility was mine, and mine alone. It was time to face my latest victim. That would be another first for me.

"No worries, Jessica. Let me go ahead and deal with this guy." I marched forward to an unknown situation. And I did so without hesitation, just as I had many times in my life. My own safety took a backseat to my obligation.

Besides, Kurt couldn't actually touch me. He was a ghost, so perhaps I didn't have much to worry about. If he needed a conversation to move on, I would gladly give it to him. Let him blame me, let him yell at me, and curse me from beyond the grave. Let him get it all out of his system. Then Pinedale Central High School would finally be done with him.

"Are you sure, Mr. Copeland?" Jessica asked. "Do you really think this is a good idea? His attitude seemed a bit...sour to me."

I looked over my shoulder and gave Jessica a reassuring smile. "I'm sure he is. Let me see what he wants."

"You're a brave man, Mr. Copeland," Jessica said.

But this wasn't about bravery; it was about logic. Taking Kurt's bait was the best move to make under the circumstances.

I reached the doorway to the lobby where I'd heard the voice. I took one last look at the hallway behind me. It was empty except for the ghost watching me with wide and worried eyes. The school was peaceful around this time, which was a big part of why I liked to hang out here after hours. Well, that was the case under normal circumstances. Today, with my name echoing off the walls, it was plain eerie. I took a deep breath and pushed open the door. No backing out. Time to face my decisions and deal with the consequences in a way I never have before.

I marched straight into the front lobby, ready to face an unknown situation. One for which I could only hope I was ready.

Chapter Eighteen

The main lobby was quiet, which was typical for this time of day. Even the one safety officer who was left after Kurt's rampage, only because he had that day off, had gone home for the day. But the lobby wasn't completely empty. The figure of a transparent ghost floating over the safety officer's circular desk caught my eye. His head slowly turned my way.

This ghost was unlike Sam or Jessica. He was far taller and more muscular, with a white smoke emanating from him, which seemed to be coming from his pores. As we made eye contact from a distance, I caught the psychotic rage on his face. His mouth formed a grimace I had seen in hardened terrorists my squad was able to capture alive and shackle. That rage was directed at me.

"I'm here, Kurt," I said, taking a slow and reluctant step forward. "I heard your call."

"Of course, you did." His voice was firm and confident; it wasn't shaky from narcotics, unlike the previous day just before he died. "I made sure my call was aimed for you."

Kurt's body turned to face me. That same white fog came from his shirt and pants as well as his skin. "Is it a coincidence that you are coming to me from the exact hallway where you killed me, Mr. Copeland?"

"That's where my office is." I shrugged and tilted

my head. "And it wasn't my intention to kill you, Kurt. I was attempting to stop the mass murder spree you were intending to commit. Innocent lives needed to be saved. From you."

The chairs in the lobby vibrated to the point they rattled. So did the huge picture windows on either side of the double doors leading to the school's front yard. Kurt slowly hovered in my direction. He looked up to the ceiling and laughed. It wasn't a friendly laugh; more so, it was one that sent a chill down my spine.

"You're new to Pinedale, aren't you?" he asked.

"I am. I've only been here a few months."

Kurt stopped in place halfway through the lobby. "Do you know that Pinedale revolves around this high school? It always has. That's not just because it's in the center of town. It's also because every event is hosted by the school." His hands rotated in a mocking way. "Pinedale Central High School supports all the youth in our community. At least, that's what our newspapers say. That's what the adults all claim. Yet, when I needed this school, and the town, to support me the most, no one was there for me."

"I'm going to need some context, Kurt." Seeing him move closer, I clenched my fists from instinct. "I have no idea what you're talking about."

His eyes widened with anger. His mouth opened, showing teeth that made him look even more psychotic than I thought possible. "That kid embarrassed me in front of everyone in the school. In that moment, I lost myself. I saw red, and then I blacked out." He let out a snort. "I don't even remember what happened next. All I knew was I was standing over him with a bunch of people holding my arms and saying he was dead. That I killed him."

"That kid's name was Sam Anderson, and you did kill him, Kurt. You strangled him until he died."

"*Not on purpose!*"

So far, this conversation had only enraged Kurt. My tactics needed to be changed, and quickly. My instincts as a soldier wouldn't help me here. Time to try some of my training as a counselor. "I hear the frustration in your voice. Talk to me about that frustration."

Kurt roared like a lion. A chair flew past me, slamming against the wall. My attempt to engage his emotions wasn't working either. So much for that technique.

"The entire town exploded over what happened, Mr. Copeland!" he shouted. "People cried! People collected money so his mother could pay for the funeral! While I was taken out in handcuffs. I sat in prison, never hearing from anybody! Not my friends, not my family, nobody! Pinedale abandoned me."

"So, your answer was to come back with a weapon and shoot up the school?"

Kurt's head turned to the far left, then to the far right. He soon refocused on me. "After all I went through, I realized that this school needed cleansing. It needed a fresh start where it is built again from the ground up with a lesson in humility. I came here to do exactly that, but you killed me, Mr. Copeland. You murdered me in cold blood, and you did it before I could have the desired effect."

I didn't need two years of education in psychology or a counseling license to realize Kurt was rambling on and had worked himself into a warped sense of reality which had festered for his entire life. His obsession was to the point where I had no chance of getting him to see the error of his actions. He was just too far gone. I needed to instead focus on the fact that Kurt was a ghost who needed to give up his existence. A back-and-forth debate on whether or not his death was justifiable wouldn't accomplish that. I had to switch tactics, and fast. Time to swallow some pride.

"Kurt, I regret killing you." I folded my hands against my chest and tried to sound as sincere as possible. "I wish there was another way. I truly do. But, in that moment, I couldn't find one. I am truly sorry. But now, you need to go."

Kurt had made his way across the lobby, coming to float in front of me. His stomach was inches from my face. He stared down at me. For a moment, I thought he was ready to accept my apology. Instead, he let out a crazy cackle. "I am not here for an apology, Mr. Copeland. Not at all."

"Then why are you here?"

Kurt raised his arms out as if he was under a spotlight. "I believe I was sent here as an angel of vengeance! I am to administer punishment to the people of Pinedale for their long-time arrogance."

"Sent?" I couldn't figure out if Kurt was still under the influence as he was when I killed him, or if anything he had just said was true. "Someone sent you, Kurt? Who sent you?"

Kurt's gaze suddenly went over my head as if he was looking to someone for an answer. "I don't know who, not exactly." His words hummed like a snake's hiss. "But I do understand my role. I get what I must do." His eyes narrowed. "And I'm starting with you. I want my retribution!'"

"Okay, Kurt." I let out a deep sigh and spread out my arms. "How, exactly, do we settle up? As far as I can tell, we're on different planes of existence. That means we can't touch one another."

Kurt lowered himself until we were face-to-face. The grin across his face concerned me. "Well, you're half right."

Kurt's right arm swung. His knuckles connected with the right side of my face. My eardrum rang as if a baseball bat had made contact. My body staggered, more from the surprise than the pain. Kurt's fist hit me solidly. If not for my back hitting the closed door behind me, I'd be on the floor flailing like a turtle. It would have been the second time in as many days Kurt knocked me into that position.

I tried to step forward but fell to my knees. My body was still reeling. "How did you…"

Kurt flew my way. "I guess one of us has more knowledge than the other on what the dead can do."

I've certainly taken harder punches, especially when I boxed in the army in my early days. But I wasn't ready for this one. I hadn't braced myself because, even though I saw it coming, I didn't think he could touch me. He fooled me, but I'm only fooled once. If Kurt could make physical contact with me, that must mean I could with him as well. I cocked my left fist and held it near my chest as I waited for his next attack. Maybe Kurt played his hand too soon. Time to play mine.

I stayed in a squatting position, feigning injury until Kurt was close enough. I waited for my opportunity, knowing I wouldn't have to wait long. From the corner of my eye, I saw him standing over me with his feet an inch from the floor. Being a southpaw gave me the advantage of surprise in many fights, both organized and in the streets. I hoped it would work this time.

Kurt reached down for my head. I jumped up and swung a hard uppercut to his jaw. My fist went straight through his face as if it was trying to hit air. Kurt threw a left jab which connected with my nose. Had I not instinctively pulled back my head, the punch could have broken some cartilage. It did, however, cause my eyes to tear up, which made everything around me blur.

I staggered back, wiping my eyes with the heel of my hand. My vision cleared in time to see a chair fly across the room, aimed for my head. I ducked and rolled out of the way. The chair shattered into pieces against the solid metal door. It was a temporary reprieve because somehow, this ghost was able to make physical contact, both with me and with inanimate objects. What made it worse was how he could toss any piece of furniture without being near it. I saw one option available to me. I hated to do it, but it was time for a hasty retreat.

The double doors which led to the outside were closed. If I could just get there, yank one open, and throw myself outside before Kurt could catch me, I would be free. This was assuming Kurt couldn't follow me outside the school just like Sam couldn't. I had to take that chance. I lunged for the door halfway across the lobby, but Kurt flew in my path. He launched both of his palms against my chest, nearly knocking the wind out of me.

Five fingers and a thumb wrapped around my throat and squeezed. I lunged my hands at Kurt's wrist, but they passed straight through. His grip tightened. I slowly breathed through my nose to conserve whatever air I had left, but it was a temporary fix at best. If I couldn't touch him, there was no way I could escape him. I needed to think of a new plan. So far, I had nothing. His annoying cackle didn't help me think.

"Let's go for a ride," Kurt said, between laughs.

My feet no longer touched the floor. We were moving toward the ceiling which meant Kurt was pulling my body—by the throat—straight up. Just my luck; the rules of physics apparently didn't translate into the afterlife. I was around two hundred and twenty pounds, yet he held me in the air with ease as if I was an infant child.

"You want to hear something funny?" Kurt leaned in so we were human eye to transparent eye. "When I was walked out of this building in cuffs, I didn't even know how to fight. I had no idea how to hurt someone. Well, not including the situation with Sam."

I took another swipe at Kurt's arm. Same result. It was like he wasn't even there, except the vise around my throat told me otherwise.

"I wasn't all that big and strong, not compared to the other inmates. But look at me now!" Kurt's eyes darkened with rage. "Amazing what two years in juvie and sixteen years in a hardcore prison will do, right, Mr. Copeland? After fight after fight—many times with multiple gang members—you learn what parts of the face to hit which will cause the most pain. Here, let me show you!"

Kurt raised a tight fist over his head. It was in line with my right cheekbone. I closed my eyes and prepared for what I expected would be a powerful and painful blow. He let out a scream, but his arm didn't drop down like a hammer as I expected. I peeked up to see another, far thinner, transparent hand wrapped around his wrist. Kurt looked over his shoulder with surprise at who he saw. He looked as stunned as I was.

"No!" Jessica screamed. "Let him go!"

Chapter Nineteen

Kurt drove his arm forward, which hurled Jessica across the room. Her body flipped in the air, over my head before she regained control and spun herself upright. At least Kurt's grip of my throat loosened. I fell to the floor, landing on my feet, coughing and gagging. Kurt flew past me. His attention was now on Jessica. That didn't mean I was out of trouble. It just meant I had a reprieve. A moment to figure out how to take advantage of it, and fast.

I had a clear path to the front doors. But leaving was no longer an option to consider. I wouldn't run for safety while leaving this petite, yet brave, girl to face a sociopathic monster by herself. No, my indecisiveness was replaced with resolve. I wasn't leaving until Kurt was stopped, or I was also among the dead.

"You aren't my target, little girl. You're already dead," Kurt growled, as he approached Jessica. "But if you insist on getting in my way, I wonder, can I harm another ghost? Let's find out."

"No!" Jessica met Kurt in the air, her eyes narrowed with anger. "I was pushed around enough while I was alive. I will not be bullied in my afterlife as well!"

Jessica swung her right hand. Her slap connected with Kurt's cheek. It stunned him, but barely. Kurt snatched a handful of her hair and yanked, forcing her body to drift near the floor. Kurt stared down at her with clenched fists and a look of rage on his face. She peered up at him with wide eyes and a shaky lower jaw. Her fear was understandable—Kurt had a height, weight, and intensity advantage over this skinny young ghost.

My instincts to protect an innocent victim took over. I dashed across the lobby and leapt at Kurt with both my arms out, looking to tackle him to the floor. A dumb move, perhaps, but if I could catch him by surprise—no, I passed straight through him, never making contact. I spun like a top, stamping my foot like a brake pedal and faced Kurt, ready to dodge whatever assault he'd throw my way.

Kurt raised his arms. The circular desk behind him rattled, as did the items on its surface. Jessica floated in front of him. She must have caught his attention because the shaking stopped. But it did cost her, Kurt swung a backhand which knocked her through the floor and into whichever room sat underneath the lobby. His angry eyes once again locked onto mine.

"Isn't it funny?" he said through a laugh. "They call this place 'Haunted High School,' and it sure haunted me for years. Now, I'm going to haunt it for the rest of eternity."

Kurt's head spun back and forth as if he was lost in the thoughts of his diabolical plans. He seemed to have forgotten about me, at least for the moment. I nearly jumped out of my skin when a head popped out from the floor directly in front of me. It was Jessica's.

I dropped down to one knee next to her. "Jessica," I whispered. "How the hell can he touch me?"

"I swear to you, Mr. Copeland, I don't know." Her

sob was far above a whisper. "I've never been able to touch any of the living, or any object."

I waved a hand toward Kurt. "But you can touch *him*."

"I was surprised as well." Jessica's body levitated from beneath the floor. "This is all new for me. I've never met another ghost, not until—"

"*Heads up!*"

A monitor from the circular desk flew my way. I dropped onto my stomach and rolled. I heard the crash of the glass screen against the wall. Jessica lifted her head. I did as well. Kurt sailed above us.

He raised his right hand and gestured at the two front doors, both of which slowly crept open. "Mr. Copeland." The tone of his voice calmed to a far less creepy volume. "I've changed my mind. I'm going to let you leave, but don't ever come back here. I give you your freedom so you can watch me tear this place to the ground, and there won't be a damn thing you can do about it."

"What about me, you monster?" Jessica hissed.

Sparks which sounded like kernels forming into popcorn shot out around Kurt. "I can't kill you, little girl, because you're already dead. But, since you're trapped here with me, you get to see what I do to this place firsthand!" His eyes widened with determination. "I suggest you stay far out of my way. I don't have to hurt you, but if you make me, I will."

Jessica's transparent body shot up in the air. "You are nothing more than a bully. A hooligan!"

"No!" Kurt pulled back a fist, forcing Jessica to stop short. "I was the one bullied! By the people of this town, and specifically, by the ones who worked in this school! Now, look at me. I'm a damned ghost!"

Kurt's eyes rolled toward the ceiling. It was as if he was listening to someone. From the frown on his face, he was being scolded. "I'm doing it!" he shouted. "Let me handle this!" Was he talking to someone, or did schizophrenia follow him beyond his death?

"Mr. Copeland." Jessica flew down to my side. "What do we do?"

I opened my mouth to offer Jessica an answer. But I had nothing. I hadn't known Kurt as a kid other than how Sam described him, which was an obnoxious, arrogant jerk. It looked like, as an adult ghost, he was still that. But, unlike most bullies, Kurt had the power to back up his threats. I recalled the anxiety I felt on my first few missions as part of my special ops unit. We were warned by our superiors that they'd deny any knowledge of us if we were killed or captured. We were on our own. Those missions proved successful, and that was the last time I ever felt that sort of pressure in my forehead. Until this moment.

I couldn't think of a way to stop this threat. The two double doors were left open, and they looked enticing. I could run out of here and this would no longer be my problem. Except I had committed myself to not abandoning Jessica, or this school, to Kurt. But if I stayed, what could I do to an enemy I couldn't touch? Jessica could touch him, but she didn't have the strength or ability to harm him, let alone take him down.

I flashed back to Sam and the stories he told me about Kurt. I was glad he moved on from being a ghost when he did. If not, he would be here having to face his bully—now a grown adult. It would have been horrible.

Kurt would have been able to touch him, just as he could Jessica. Just as he could me. If only I could defend myself—

Wait! Sam had possessed Lieutenant Banks. He was able to physically touch things while in that body. Was it possible…I was sure no ghost expert, as both Sam and Jessica liked to say, but it was worth a shot. In fact, it may be our only chance.

"Jessica." I spun my head her way. "Can you possess my body but not my brain?"

She did a doubletake. "Can I what?"

"Enter my body but let me drive. Can you do that?"

"I have no idea. I've never gone into the living before. I do mean never."

"Sam did it!" My revelation made her eyes open wide. "That means you can, too. Try!"

Jessica floated up to me, and then her ethereal form oozed into me. Her body disappeared as it phased inside mine. First, I grew lightheaded. Then a wave of euphoria filled my body as my vision momentarily blurred. It felt like I was high except I had no drugs in my system. The sensation cleared, but something was different; I heard static inside my brain behind my own thoughts. I lifted my foot and stepped forward. It took an extra moment for the touch of the floor against the sole of my black shoe to register.

The euphoria lessened, but it wasn't gone. In that moment, I was me, but I was also her. It was almost like being in a dream state, except I was fully aware of myself and my actions. My chest was tight, like a hand was pressing against my heart. It was anxiety, but not my own. It was coming from Jessica.

"Kurt!" I shouted. "We're' not done speaking yet!"

"Mr. Copeland!" Kurt's attention pulled from the ceiling. He glared at me while lowering himself to the floor. "It looks like the girl ghost took off. She's smart. I don't get why you're still here."

"I'm not going anywhere!" I stretched out my arms to show myself off. "I think you're the one leaving, punk!"

Kurt's chuckle turned into an ear-splitting cackle. "Okay then. Don't say I didn't give you the chance to walk out of here, right?"

Kurt flew at me with both fists pointed forward. I closed my left hand and held it tight. I waited for him to come close. His right hand pulled back and aimed for my head. I ducked the wild swing, feeling a slight satisfaction that, this time, it was Kurt who hit nothing but air. I slammed my fist against his jaw with a strong straight cross. I felt something solid against my knuckles. Kurt clutched his jaw. His body sailed backward. I'm not so sure I hurt him all that bad, but his wide-eyed expression meant, at the very least, I confused him.

"I...I don't get it." Kurt clutched at his jaw. His hand passed straight through. "I know I can hit you but...how—"

"Yeah, you really kicked my ass." I grinned with renewed self-confidence. "My turn, now."

Chapter Twenty

Another hard left backed Kurt out of my personal space. He was staggered and still stunned over the fact that I could touch him. That meant I had to take advantage as quickly as I could before Kurt got his bearings. I had a few moments at best. Hopefully, it would be enough.

He screamed in rage, then flew at me. This time, I was ready. I grabbed his right arm in mid-swing and used his momentum to throw Kurt's ghostly body across the room. He spun in midair and flew at me again. This time, I sidestepped him and blasted a knee into his stomach, stopping the ghost in his tracks. That allowed me to slip behind Kurt and wrap my right arm across his throat. I grabbed my wrist with my left hand so I could squeeze tight enough to cut off his windpipe.

"What do you think you're doing?" Kurt laughed. "You can't choke me, I'm a ghost!"

"He's right, Mr. Copeland," Jessica said, inside my head. It sounded like my own thoughts, except it was in her voice. "We don't need to breathe; we're already dead."

Damn me for not realizing that on my own. I released my grip and pushed Kurt forward. Once he spun around, I ran at full speed and rammed him into the wall. Kurt raised his hands in fear at the sight of my left fist flying his way.

Jessica's cheers rang between my ears. "Yes! Put him down, Mr. Copeland!"

Before my fist could connect with his nose, Kurt recoiled until he disappeared through the wall. I touched the solid wall. I couldn't pass through it even with a ghost inside of me. Was the fight over? Did Kurt tuck tail and run?

No such luck. Kurt suddenly shot out from the wall and tagged me with a right fist to my cheek.

"Ooh, I felt that!" Jessica cried. "I believe you did, as well."

I shook off the blow to my face, then swung with what I hoped would be a knockout punch. Kurt's body dropped straight through the floor. "Dammit!" I shouted, looking back and forth with my fists clenched. He had to come up eventually—

My legs pulled out from under me. I fell forward like a tree that had been cut down. On instinct, I raised my hands forward, just barely keeping my face from splattering all over the floor. Jessica screeched in my head, "Mr. Copeland, are you okay?" She was so loud, I thought my brain would pop like a balloon.

"I'm fine," I muttered. "Let me focus."

Kurt had his bearings; he adapted to the situation. My window of advantage had passed, and he once again had the upper hand. Kurt was handling himself like an experienced pro, not like someone who had just become a ghost within the last twenty-four hours. Someone else must be pulling those strings, but there wasn't time to ponder that, not yet.

I pushed against the floor to get my head straight. Then I pulled my feet under my body, getting myself into a squatting position. I picked my head up to find

Kurt floating over me. His foot slammed against my forehead. For a moment, I saw stars. I needed some distance from Kurt, and I needed it fast.

I rolled away, ignoring the stinging sensation across my right cheekbone. Then I hopped to my knees with my left arm in a defensive position. With my right hand, I touched the side of my face. My fingers picked up a smear of blood. Mine.

"You really should have left when I gave you the chance," Kurt squawked. "Now, you have to pay, just like this entire school has to pay!"

I threw out my left leg, aiming my heel at his shin. It was a move from my lessons on how to take down an opponent standing over me, much like Kurt was doing. I practiced it so often, it became instinct. Unfortunately, while those instincts were still sharp, my older body had lost some of its speed. Kurt levitated in the air and out of reach before I could connect.

"Mr. Copeland!" Jessica's voice popped into my head again. "He's beating us. Badly. What do we do?"

"Give me a minute to think."

"I don't think we have a minute."

My head lifted, and not by my own will. Jessica was right. Kurt had lowered himself inches from the floor and he stared at me with a look I had seen in the eyes of enemy soldiers who had targeted me for a body bag. Maybe getting out of the school was my best strategic move, after all. But it was too late.

Then again, maybe it wasn't. The double doors leading to the outside were still wide open, offering me an escape to salvation. All I had to do was get past Kurt. I knew he wouldn't make it easy, but I had the skills to at least make my way past him, even if I couldn't outright beat him. I hated to bail on everyone, especially Jessica who wouldn't be able to leave with me. She gave me this chance to fight. But maybe it was best to live to fight another day—

My mind flashed to Sam and all the attempts he made in front of me to escape the confines of the school. Each time, he bounced back as if he had run straight into a trampoline. Jessica never left either, which meant she also couldn't without suffering the same barrier that would shoot her back. Would those same "ghost rules" apply to Kurt even though he was far stronger than either of them? Time to find out.

I rose to my feet and waved Kurt to come at me. "Mr. Copeland, what are you doing?" Jessica asked.

"Just stay inside of me," I demanded. "I have an idea."

My bravado sparked another laugh from the ghost in front of me. "Are you joking?" Kurt spread his arms, displaying his disbelief. "What do you think you're going to do when I can stick and move until your mortal body tires out—"

I ran at Kurt, ramming my shoulder into his gut, and wrapping my hands around his waist. I rushed for the open doorway, taking Kurt with me. "What do you think you're doing?" he screeched.

As soon as we were close, I stopped short and let Kurt go. He flew backward into the open doorway. Just like Sam, his body jolted, and bounced right at me. I hit him in the cheekbone with a left cross, then shoved him back. The same thing happened; his body shook, then he flew forward. Before he could react, I ran at him with both hands again into the open doorway.

Kurt's arms and legs flailed. I could have played

ping-pong with him all day, but this time, I charged and slammed my forearm against Kurt's chest, sandwiching him between me and the outside. I felt the pressure in my arm of the force trying to send Kurt back, but I planted my feet and stood my ground. Kurt's body shook like a struck tuning fork. It was as if he was suffering an epileptic seizure.

My insides shook. "Mr. Copeland!" Jessica screamed in my head. "What you're doing...I feel the vibration...it's trying...to force me back as well!"

"Fight it, Jessica! Stay inside me!" I pushed forward with my entire body, refusing to lose my ground.

"It's working, Mr. Copeland," Jessica said. "But he's tearing apart. He's suffering—"

Kurt's body vibrated against my arm. His high-pitched screech reflected his pain. "P...p...ple...ase..." His lower jaw jittered to the point I thought it may rip off his face.

I felt Jessica's panic inside me. "Mr. Copeland! How long—"

"Wait!" My own voice quaked from the vibration emanating from Kurt.

I gave it another few seconds, then jumped out of the way. Kurt propelled forward. His body flipped twice in the air. He landed close to the floor, on his knees. I stepped in front of him. Kurt's head pointed downward. His hands and feet were still trembling. So was his jaw. My fists were clenched even though I was sure Kurt was no longer a threat.

Jessica leaped out of my body. The sensation of a ghost leaving me caused a hell of a headache. I almost lost my balance, but I was determined to stay on my feet and push the dizziness aside. There would be plenty of time to recover later. At least my feelings were all my own; there was no one else inside my body.

I stood over Kurt and waited until he looked up at me. It didn't take long. His widened transparent eyes locked onto mine. "We know how to take you out, Kurt, we know how to beat you. That means this school is no longer your hostage. Your mission is over. You've lost. You're done."

"I get it, man, I really do." Kurt pulled back his head. His feet dropped straight through the floor. "None of this was my idea, I swear. I-I just want to go, that's all."

"Well, I'll be darned," Jessica said from behind me. "We really did win."

Unlike with Jessica, Kurt's response didn't surprise me at all. Like any typical bully, once they're shown up or scared, they fall apart, cower, then plead for escape. In this moment, I wanted to grant him his wish and let him go. Or pummel him some more. But neither was an option, at least not yet. I still had questions.

"You're not going anywhere, Kurt. First, I want an answer." I dropped to one knee so I could be eye-to-eye with his ghost. "You said someone sent you here. Who?"

"Never saw him. But he's powerful. So nasty." Kurt's words slurred. His body still trembled. At least his angry power trip had deescalated. "He hates this place even more than I do."

"Who is it, Kurt?" I leaned in and gave him my most intimidating glare. "Tell me. Now."

His head shook. "It doesn't matter."

"*What's his name?*" I said with a raised voice.

"I…I can't," he cried. "I'm sorry."

Damn, I wasn't going to get anywhere with him. Whoever was pulling the strings scared Kurt a hell of a lot more than I ever could. But one threat at a time, and the threat in front of me was Kurt Baker.

"Listen carefully." I leaned in so close my nose passed through his. The fact that he leaned back meant I had him spooked. The irony wasn't lost on me. "You're done haunting Pinedale High. You need to go. It's time for you to move on from this plane of existence."

I stood up and stared down at Kurt. He still wore a slight defiance in his eyes, but after a glance at the open doors, he faded away in much the same way as Sam. I allowed myself a moment to slouch. I used the back of my hand to rub the blood running down my right cheek.

"You did it," Jessica squealed.

"We did it, Jessica," I said, through a deep sigh. "We beat him. He's gone."

"Yes, we did—" Her voice cut off mid-sentence.

I looked to my left and to my right. Then I spun around and scanned the entire lobby. Jessica was gone as well. As far as I knew, I was the only one here, both living and dead. Maybe Jessica needed this victory to enter the peaceful slumber of death? Was Kurt gone, or did he just make a strategic retreat? Maybe neither of them had moved on and were still somewhere in this school. I couldn't know because, like Jessica, I wasn't a ghost expert.

But I was sure I knew someone with more expertise on the subject than anyone else realized. Luckily, I had an idea where to find him at this time of the early evening.

I had promised myself I would make time to speak with him again. Now was that time.

Chapter Twenty-one

I walked a few blocks to the diner's parking lot. "Lou's", in huge letters, blinked above the door's awning. Sure enough, the vehicle I expected to see was there. I saw it in the lot just about every day when I passed on my way home at this time. It was an old station wagon with more rust than red paint and looked like it had at least a few hundred thousand miles on it. Time to head into the diner.

The bells attached to the glass door clanged as I entered. The place was huge with a long counter that reminded me of the old-fashioned style diners from 1960's television sitcoms. The booths had little jukeboxes that took a quarter to choose a song. Those songs played on the speakers hanging high on the walls.

I paused at the sight of the redheaded teenage boy who froze in place at the sight of me as he was looking to exit the diner. "Mr. Copeland," he gasped. "Um, what are ya doing here?"

"Same as you, Rex," I answered. "Grabbing some supper."

Rex peeked over his shoulder at the adult couple standing behind him, holding hands. The woman's hair was full of red dye which matched her low-cut red blouse. The gentleman with the short blond hair sported a wrinkled white shirt and blue tie that suggested he took his family to dinner after a long and hard day at work. I guessed both were in their early forties.

"So, you're Mr. Copeland, the new guidance counselor at Pinedale." The man held out his hand for me to shake. "I'm Todd Sullivan, This is my wife, Paige. We're Rex's parents."

Todd's hand jerked back. He looked over my face with widened eyes. "Hard day?" he asked.

"I had an accident doing some construction on my home. I decided I needed a break." I accepted his handshake, then shook his wife's hand as well. "It's nice to meet you both."

"How's Rex doing in school?" Paige asked. "I do hope we he's not giving you too much trouble."

Rex threw me a nervous glance that his parents didn't catch. His Adam's apple rolled down his throat. "He's doing okay." I returned Rex's glance with a slight smirk. "And I'm sure he's working hard to do even better. Right, Rex?"

"Uh, yeah, for sure," he answered, through a relieved gulp.

"That's good to hear," Paige replied.

"If he ever falls off track, or you need anything, please let us know." Todd gave my arm a playful slap. "It's nice meeting you, Mr. Copeland. Enjoy your supper."

Paige's gaze shot to my forehead. "You might want to put some ice on that," she said with concern.

"I'll do that, Mrs. Sullivan. Thank you."

I stepped aside so the three could leave. Rex breathed a sigh of relief as he passed by me. His eyes thanked me for my silence. I had to admit, there was a sense of power in making the kid sweat. He now owed me one, and it was good to have something over the toughest student in the school.

A quick glance around the diner led me to the man I'd come to see. Hank sat at a booth in the back of the diner, alone with an open newspaper on the table in front of him. He still wore his dirty custodial overalls. The waitress, a tall lady with curled dark brown hair and an apron over her uniform skirt, strolled to the table.

"Hey, Laura." Hank looked up with a smile.

"Hey, yourself, Hank. You here for your usual?"

"Absolutely!" Hank clapped his hands together. "With a cup of coffee, black." "Okay, one plate of fresh fruit you'll barely touch and a cup of coffee you'll hardly drink." Laura smirked while writing the order on a pad with her pencil. "You do realize the chef looks at me funny every time I place this order, then bring back the full plate?"

"What can I say, Laura?" Hank laughed. "The fruit reminds me of my youth, and I love the smell of fresh roast in the early morning."

Laura peeked at her watch. "Or at five thirty in the early evening," she snickered.

Hank shrugged. "Hey, it must be early morning somewhere in the world, wouldn't you say?"

"I suppose that's true." Laura dropped the pad with her pencil into her apron pocket. "Let me go grab that order for you, Hank."

I walked up to the table and stood next to the waitress on her left. My sudden appearance must have caught Hank by surprise based on the double take he gave me. "Tell you what, Laura, let me get a cheeseburger, fries, and a diet cola. Put both meals on my bill."

165

"You got it." She scribbled on her pad one more time, then shuffled off, leaving me standing alone in front of the booth. My eyes locked with Hank's, who stared up at me from his seated position. He had a look of confusion and concern.

"Those are some serious bruises all over your face, Mr. Copeland." His head pulled back. "So, to what do I owe this free meal?"

I sat across the table from Hank. "You and I need to talk, my friend."

"Do you have a specific topic you want to converse over?" His elbows leaned against the table.

"I do. Ghosts."

"I thought we spoke on that already in the morning, Mr. Copeland." Hank closed the newspaper. "You told me you met one."

"Three ghosts, Hank; two of them, I met today." I took a deep breath to calm myself. I knew I had no reason to be flippant, but I wanted him to be a lot more forthcoming. I wasn't accepting any less. "Today, I dealt with a girl ghost named Jessica and Kurt Baker!"

"Kurt Baker? The shooter?" Hank leaned back. "I didn't know he became a ghost, too."

"He did, and he was able to make physical contact with me." I circled my finger around my face. "Anything you'd like to share on this subject, Hank? Because I really need to know what the hell is going on in our school."

The man's fingers tapped the table. I barely noticed the chimes from the front door opening. Not until the newest customer approached our table. "Good evening, gentlemen. I do hope I am not interrupting."

"Principal Kouriki." A suspicious bell went off in

my head that her friendly greeting was more than just her saying hello to two subordinates she happened to come across. "You look like you have something on your mind."

"I do, Mr. Copeland. To be honest, I was planning to grab my supper, then stop by your place so we could speak. But, as it turns out, you're here. I do hope you have the time now since it is a topic of utmost importance."

Damn, I really didn't want to get sidetracked from my conversation with Hank. Whatever issue she needed to address with me, it couldn't have been more important. But she must have thought it was significant enough to track me down tonight instead of waiting until the morning at work.

I let out a defeated sigh. "What do you wish to speak about, Principal Kouriki?"

"The new state-of-the-art surveillance cameras I had installed in our school a few years back."

"I'm afraid I don't understand." Or grasp what the cameras had to do with me, or why this was such an important topic for her.

Kouriki sat next to me. I moved in to give her some room even though she wasn't exactly invited. "During the school days, they run non-stop. But, after the school day, they only turn on when the motion sensors are activated. As they did this afternoon."

My eyebrows rose. "That's some expensive technology you put in the school."

"That it is," she said with pride. "But I felt they were important. I've been trying to find evidence to collaborate rumors within my school. Today, I think a few of my cameras may have picked up just that."

"I'm still not understanding. Rumors of what?"

"My tablet at home is synced to the computer system so when they go off, I can view what they are picking up." Her body shifted so she could face me. "What I saw around an hour ago, was my counselor in the lobby, throwing wild punches at someone who wasn't there. The entire time, I saw your lips moving, meaning you were in conversation, yet you were all alone."

"You saw that?" Damn, those pesky cameras caught me again.

She gave me a knowing nod. "At first, I thought you were having some sort of psychotic episode. You are, after all, a veteran who has seen some pretty nasty things, as I have recently learned."

"Principal Kouriki—"

She raised her finger, cutting me off. "But, I watched two chairs and a computer monitor lift in the air and fly at you. Then I saw you get thrown around like a beanbag by someone I could not see."

"No kidding?" Hank pointed at my face. "Okay, that does explain where the bruises came from."

"After seeing that, I rewatched the video of your confrontation with Kurt Baker," she went on.

"I thought that footage was erased."

"On the FBI's database, I'm sure it was. But not before I saved it on my personal tablet. I played it from the part where Kurt looked distracted, which was before you tussled with him over the gun." She threw me a sideways glance, one that was accompanied by a slight grin. "The lieutenant and the detective noticed Kurt was distracted, which you explained away quite nicely. But what they didn't notice, and I did, was afterward where you were speaking to someone even though no one else was there. I'm sure, had the agents who visited us yesterday caught it, they wouldn't have given it much thought. Of course, they also weren't privy to all the claims of ghost sightings within those walls."

"I'm guessing you have a theory?" I saw it in her eyes. They weren't filled with curiosity.

"More like questions, Mr. Copeland." Kouriki faced me and leaned her left elbow on the table. Her fist pressed against her cheek. "I have overheard claims of ten ghost sightings by students at Pinedale High as far back as when I was a young teacher. I've never seen one, and none of the staff have—at least none have come forward. But I have witnessed enough aftermath that I couldn't explain. I've seen windows broken and tables knocked over during the night hours when no one was in the building. I've seen tough students who were spooked. I cannot contemplate what I saw in those videos, Mr. Copeland. So, for the sake of my own sanity, I'm hoping you can offer some clarity."

"I see."

I could have explained yesterday away by saying I was talking to Kurt's corpse, but I couldn't defend what she saw about an hour ago. Even if I could, I knew the expression on her face well. I had seen it on people far more powerful. Kouriki had a goal that she was determined to achieve, and she wouldn't let anything stop her. I had no doubt her fortitude led her to becoming principal. If I tried to avoid the subject or chose to not answer, this woman would not give up. She'd become relentless; that was her nature. It was time to bring her in.

"I don't know if I can explain what's going on in

our school, Principal Kouriki." I looked across the table at Hank. "But I have a hunch he can. That's why I'm here talking to Hank. I want the same answers."

"Is that true, Hank?" Kouriki asked. "Do you have the insight we're looking for?"

Hank shrugged. "I may have seen and heard a lot in my time at Pinedale High. Not that anyone ever wants to listen to the custodian, right?"

Hank laughed. Kouriki and I did not. "We're listening to you now, Hank," I said with as much sincerity as I could show. "Talk to us. Please."

"If I do share what I know," Hank replied, "and we pool all of our knowledge together, figure it all out. What will we do with this information?"

It was a good question. I hadn't thought that far ahead. "I don't know. I guess we'd have to warn the world that we have a building filled with ghosts. Maybe bring in some help—"

"That is a terrible plan!" Kouriki cut me off.

Laura returned to the table with a tray of food balanced across her arm. She laid one plate of fruit in front of Hank and the other plate with a cheeseburger and fries in front of me. "Here ya go, guys," she said while placing the glass of soda and the steaming cup of coffee on the table. She then said to Kouriki, "Your order is just about ready for pick up, Ma'am."

"Change of plans, Laura." Kouriki smacked the table. "I'm going to eat here."

"Understood. One house special salad with grilled chicken on top and an iced tea, to stay. Both are on their way."

Kouriki watched Laura head behind the counter and then through the doors leading to the kitchen. She turned her attention back to us.

"Taking this public would destroy Pinedale High's reputation," Kouriki explained. "Parents would never send their children to a building they know is haunted. It could even lead to families leaving Pinedale in droves. No, we need to keep this between us and handle it internally, however we can."

"Agreed." Hank clenched his hand into a fist and shook it.

Both sets of eyes fell on me. I didn't love the idea. There were a lot of ways our trying to handle a situation like this could blow up in our faces. But Kouriki did have a point. Ahh, what the hell? "Okay, agreed."

"Good." Kouriki peeked around, perhaps making sure the coast was clear. She then returned her attention to us. "Okay, gentlemen, tell me what you know about the hauntings of Pinedale High."

A word about the author...

By day, Mark Rosendorf is a mild-mannered guidance counselor in the New York City school system's special education district. He is also a former professional magician.

But, by night, Mark is the proud author of the award-winning series, "The Witches of Vegas," a five-book set which includes *The Witches of Vegas*, *Journey to New Salem, Witch's Gamble, Witch Way to Vegas*, and *Wiccan Mirror*. The Witches of Vegas series has won many awards including the prestigious RONE award, The Pencraft award for literary excellence, The Critter's annual reader's poll, and several others.

Mark is happily married and living in Queens, New York. Make sure to check out his website, http://markrosendorf.com

Thank you for purchasing
this publication of The Wild Rose Press, Inc.

For questions or more information
contact us at
info@thewildrosepress.com.

The Wild Rose Press, Inc.
www.thewildrosepress.com